The Sword of the Gray Queen 2:

Hive of the Formicae

Samuel Fleming

Cover Art by MiblArt

ISBN-13: 978-1-954679-56-6 (paperback)
ISBN-13: 978-1-954679-55-9 (ebook)

For Mom and Dad.

Thanks for always supporting me

and believing in me.

Contents

"There are many creatures that prey on the mortal plane: The Corrupted, the Faceless, and the Demon-Blooded. They are the antithesis to the Light, and thrive in Darkness. If they take foothold, bear no pause, nor pity, nor malice as you strike down the tainted—for if they were righteous or innocent, they are no longer."
—ENCHIRIDION:
Quod Intus Viget Tenebris.
First Tenants, Chapter 1.

Prologue

SANTA ANNA STARED out the carriage window. In the distance, the mountain of Plaidosa receded into the fog. She'd been there two months, excavating the ruins of the Mecendu civilization.

Two months—it was hard to believe it had only been that long.

Now, she was shackled and heading for the coast. From there, they would take her from the Frozen Isles across the Gelid Sea, back to Eadruin. Back to the Church.

The two guards sitting opposite her in the carriage kept glancing at the metal gloves that enclosed her hands. They were young and tense. Scared.

Anna suppressed a smirk. *Good*, she thought. They should be scared. And not because of her, or the magic that she could loose upon them.

No. They should be scared that the Church had ordered her to stop her research. That they sent knights to apprehend her and bring her back like she was a criminal—that they ordered her silence.

The Church was scared of what she might find in the ruins of Mecendu.

The columen would want a report of what she had found. Then they would decide what to do with her.

Instead of dwelling on the inevitable, Santa Anna turned her thoughts toward what she had control over. She mentally counted her allies. Even as a Saint and a columen, she trusted precious few in the Church. Her apprehension and return in chains meant that the columen had unanimously voted for her return. Which meant that she had no allies left among her brethren.

Thankfully, she had a few archleon and priests that would take her word, and a few outside the Church as well. She thought of Kevril Bersk, the former Knight of Kripishi. She would need him, and stifled a smile.

If Santa Anna was right about the return of Ariazi, the mother of all demons, then they would need all the help they could get.

~ ~ ~

Chapter 1
The Wake of the Proud

THE RAVEN, ARCHIMEDES, swept through the trees like a ghost. Kevril Bersk watched through its eyes.

Two days he'd been hunting the fey, and he was getting close. Close enough to find fresh kills and shed fur that glistened orange.

The hunter trudged through the thick underbrush, nothing more than a flicker of steel and shadow of leather, occasionally calling *Twitch* to his gloved right hand. The glistening blue sword was almost an afterthought—appearing and disappearing as quickly as a thought.

The morning air was cool, and his muscles burned dully from the trek. Bersk relished it, resisting the temptation to use magic to ease the journey. It was better this way. The dull burn, methodical steps, and occasional sword swings gave his mind something to focus on—rather that, than to quiet such things and stew in his own thoughts.

There was always the option of merging with Archimedes and flying within the raven's body, but the thought made Bersk shudder. It was possible, but most unpleasant, even for short journeys. It was disorienting, nauseating, and left Bersk feeling *icky*—even for extremely short durations. It was a desperate power reserved for escapes and dire infiltrations, only. And so, totally out of the question.

Slow and steady, Bersk reminded himself. Humans couldn't run faster than most creatures—in fact, a human without magic was pitiful compared to most in terms of speed. But given a long enough chase, even an unaided human could outlast most prey. Even fey gods.

In that, Bersk had faith.

~

When the morning cool was nearly gone, Archimedes caught a glimpse of the fey. Its jagged antlers tore at the saplings while it lumbered through the underbrush like an orange bear.

Sometime later, it curled into a dark thicket of bramble. The vines twisted around its antlers as the fey turned around and around, settling down to sleep through the midday sun. Magic seeped around the thicket, and the brown antlers seemed to melt into the vegetation.

A normal person could walk right by the thicket without seeing the slumbering god—assuming the fey didn't decide to eat them.

But then Kevril Bersk wasn't a normal man and Archimedes wasn't a normal bird.

Its avoidance of daylight narrowed down the origin of the beast considerably. Somehow it had gotten lost, away from whatever dense forest had been its home.

Bersk continued bushwacking toward his prey and considered his options: Fey were mostly intelligent and could speak, though their thoughts were closer to that of beasts than humans. There was a chance it could be reasoned with. Perhaps even directed back toward its home.

But if it was crazed, then Bersk's options narrowed considerably.

Some gods were bound to a place. Most fey were bound to forests. If this one was gone too long from its home, well…

There was always the blade.

~

It was mid-afternoon when Bersk reached the fey's hiding spot. He contemplated hiding his footsteps with a silence spell, but decided against it. He had to hope that the fey god could be reasoned with. And sneaking up on it with sword drawn and veiled with magic would not give a good first impression.

So Kevril Bersk bushwacked until he was twenty feet away, then found a clearing before the thicket. There he stood and willed away his sword. "*Vires et voluntatem*," Bersk whispered. Strength flowed into his muscles and hardened his bones.

Then he said aloud, "My name is Kevril Bersk. I know you dwell in the thicket, fey god. I beseech you to talk."

The thicket stirred, rustling as if a dozen deer might bolt from it, but only one solitary pair of antlers rose through the bramble. They towered over Bersk, some ten feet in the air. The fey turned, and Bersk felt the ground shake with each step.

Even from afar and half-hidden, it smelled like berries and charcoal.

From behind the bramble, two eyes peered back, a swirl of bright green and bloodshot red.

It sniffed the air, then glanced upward to where Archimedes perched high above them, before turning back to Kevril.

The fey god spoke in a voice that was a mix of gentle wind and snapping branches. "Kevril Bersk, who believes he is the son of Geof and Eisha. Why do you follow me?"

Bersk ignored the insult. "You're a long way from home. You've killed livestock and destroyed property. Do you remember?"

The stained emerald eyes stared back, unblinking. "I remember." Its mouth barely moved as it spoke.

"Where are you from?"

"Odhran. The ironwood forest..."

Bersk sighed and rubbed his temples.

"Where is Odhran?" the fey asked.

"It's... hard to explain," Bersk replied uneasily. "Fey, would you step out of the thicket?"

"So you can kill me? You are warded for battle."

Bersk corrected, "So I can help you. You are tainted and unwell. I hold no weapons."

The god sneered, "You *have* no weapons."

Bersk narrowed his eyes. "Just because you do not see a sword, doesn't mean it's not within my grasp, fey god. Now, step into the light so that I can help you."

The fey stepped forward, its head, shoulders, and forelimbs appearing from the bramble. Its antlers towered over Bersk. Its head was that of a deer, but the skin of its jaw was shredded...and the teeth extended too far back in its mouth, resembling that of a crocodile rather than a deer. Its shoulders and limbs were bulky, as if the muscles of a bear had swollen and begun losing fur.

But the hands... the hands nearly made Bersk's jaw hang open. The hairless arms of the fey ended in giant, human hands—the fingers twitching and digging into the ground.

Bersk had seen enough tainted fey to know that this wasn't normal. Something was gravely wrong with the creature before him.

"How far away is Odhran, Kevril Bersk? I cannot feel my mother's roots."

"What is your name, fey?"

"I am Aryvon, sprout of Arietes and Odhran." The fey stared down at Bersk.

The bounty hunter stared back, palms beginning to sweat.

"The Odhran forest is miles away, Aryvon. But it feels faint because much of it was destroyed by Sircius Everdeath some twenty years ago. Do you remember?"

That question hung between them, and unbeknownst to Aryvon, it would decide the fey god's fate.

For the first time, fleeting emotion passed over the god's mangled face. The skin that was left on its cheek raised, ever so slightly.

"*Everdeath...*" the god said, its voice harsh like a falling tree. "I remember. I tried... I tried to stop him. *He did this to me.*"

Bersk sighed wearily. "Then I am sorry, Aryvon. Your fate is beyond my magic. There is only one course left."

"What is that, Kevril Bersk?"

"I must ask my goddess, the Gray Queen, to save you. But I can't promise you that it is a fate you will enjoy."

The gruesome face stared back at him, emerald eyes unblinking. Bersk counted five breaths before it answered.

"Then by your Goddess, I don't want to be a monster any-more."

Bersk nodded, then bid the fey god to lie down on the ground. Then the bounty hunter willed *Twitch* to his gloved right hand and set to the task of marking the ground surrounding the creature.

Bersk did this task warily, for the splotchy fur of the fey god bristled as he traced the ground.

~

Tracing the sigils in the grass was no easy task, but then such things came automatically to the hunter. Countless times he had drawn the squares and circles, and their proper intersecting lines. He had memorized much in his long career—spells, wards, summons, among other things.. Some called such things dedication, but Bersk knew it was something more.

He no longer worked *for* the Church or the order of Kripishi, but his life had carried on in much the same trajectory as it had before. He was a monster hunter, a bounty hunter, and still, on occasion, worked *for* Pater O'Malley and Santa Anna…

Bersk shook his head. Santa Anna was his current source of worry. She was a bishop—one of the highest ranking members of the Church—and she had been accused of *something*. Something that no one would speak of, something that sent her into hiding, and the Church desperately looking for her.

This time Anna had gone and gotten herself into serious *stercus*. And when Bersk saw her again, he was going to give her what for. Assuming—hoping—that the Church didn't kill her first.

When the bounty hunter was finished tracing the sigils of his Goddess around the fey god Aryvon, the ground was covered in arcane symbols. The task had taken so long that the fey had laid its head flat on the ground, its bright green eyes unmoving.

The bounty hunter walked around and knelt in front of the fey and the sigils.

Kevril asked, "Do you have anything you wish to say before I start?"

Aryvon lifted its mangled head. Even laying on the ground, its neck and shoulders were tall enough that Aryvon looked him in the eye.

"Only that it is a dark time when a god turns to another for aid. I have no home, no father. If your goddess wills it, I shall be in her debt and serve her as surely as if she made me."

Bersk nodded, then he held out *Twitch* over the sigils and spoke the old words:

"By the will of the Gray Queen, I am her hand and her voice.
I stand upon the shoulders of The Dead Prince,
Spurned by the Realm That Has No Name.
We impose the Balance upon this cursed fey."

When he spoke the final line, two other voices overlapped his, and Kevril Bersk knew he was not alone.

Glowing blue dripped from the sword, the consistency of molten gold. The blue ether dripped steadily and coalesced into the lines of the sigil. The glow retreated from the sword, leaving dull steel in its wake.

And when all the ether had shifted from the sword to the runes, Bersk finished the incantations.

"By the will of the Gray Queen, take away this madness from Aryvon." the three voices said.

The molten sigils began to flare and pulse, like blue fire dancing around the fey god. Fire that did not burn.

"Kevril Bersk!" Aryvon shouted—its voice harsh as trampled branches. "It burns and twists within me."

The fey deer struggled to stand, to run, but thick blue vines wrapped around its limbs, pulling its grisly human hands beneath the ground. Still, Aryvon struggled and sank farther—up to its elbows and knees. Its great antlers slashed through the saplings around and above.

"It burns!" the fey bellowed.

"Be strong, Aryvon!" Bersk said sternly. "It is not you that burns. It is Everdeath's affliction that burns—that struggles against you."

Aryvon's voice devolved into cracks and snaps.

Bersk grit his teeth. He would've spared the poor god the suffering if there was another way. He had seen—he had *felt* the cleansing fire before, but nothing eased the anguish of watching helplessly while another burned.

Slowly, Aryvon's skin grew back across its bony cheeks, its mouth grew slender like a deer. Orange fur creeped back across its skin, covering the fey. Its muscles shrank—

But the god's stature diminished, too. No longer did Aryvon look Bersk in the eye or its antlers tower over him. The fey was already half its size.

And as Bersk thought of his question, he felt the Goddess and the Dead Prince's voices mix with his own. "*Aryvon, sprout of Arietes and Odhran. The corruption has claimed too much of you, and your form cannot survive. But your essence may live in this forest, should you choose. Speak, fey.*"

In the span of moments, Aryvon was no taller than Kevril's waist. It looked up at the hunter with perfect emerald eyes, and when it spoke, its voice was quiet as the breeze.

"I choose to stay and to live, my Queen."

At once, the green light ebbed and drained down its face like weeping tears. Green and orange swirled in its fur like grass in the wind. Then the body of Aryvon slipped beneath the ground and mixed with the soil and roots.Life, in a sense. Death, too. But better than most could hope for.

The magic faded before him, the blue fire of the sigils dampening, and the smell of berries and charcoal fading.

Bersk held the sword out again over the sigil and the blue ether lept from its bounds back to the blade, coating and coloring it back to its eerie glow.

"*Order come, and Gray Queen's will be done,*" the three said.

Then Bersk felt his Goddess and the Prince leave him, and he was alone in the quiet forest—

Or nearly so. High in the treetops, Archimedes crowed with satisfaction and with reminder that the psychopomp was never far.

~ ~ ~

THE 14TH COMPANY of the citystate of Arkcaster marched across the countryside. The forests around them had begun to thin, giving way to blue sky. They were nearly at the Cliffs of Moor. They would would camp near the cliffs and then head down to the valley.

Specialist Xandra walked just ahead of the main brigade. She breathed deep. There was a part of her that missed the city—the comforting lull of foot traffic and conversation, even in the dead of night. But there was an equally large part of her that relished the wilds, these untouched, unmarred portions of the world.

Maybe it was the soldier in her that relished the quiet, weathering of the elements, and the close camaraderie. Maybe it was the hunter in her. But then—

"You're musing again." Sergeant Weylan walked beside her and smirked. "You've been doing that a lot this mission."

Xandra glanced at her confidant, and tried to hide her smile. "Shouldn't you be ordering someone around?"

Weylan shrugged. "We've had a long march. I'll order them around once we've found a spot for camp. Besides, I'd rather talk to you."

She rolled her eyes and spared herself one more glance at him. Just once more to follow the sharp lines of his jaw and his lips.

Xandra cleared her throat. "Just because Captain Henring is dense and we're away from civilization doesn't mean that we can be brazen."

The sergeant nodded, obviously dejected. "Yes, ma'am."

"Besides, we—" Xandra caught the scent of blood and she froze. "Do you smell that?"

"Yes."

Xandra called for the brigade to halt, then ordered the closest five soldiers to fan out and search the area with her and Sergeant Weylan. While the soldiers fanned out, the senior officers followed the scent through the woods and to a barren clearing.

To the right lay the cliff's rocky edge. To the left lay the mangled bodies of the forward patrol.

"To me!" Xandra yelled, drawing her blade.

~ ~ ~

Chapter 2
Sellswords and Commoners

THE HUNTER BID Archimedes to fly high in the sky and look for the nearest town. Luckily, there was a village in the direction of the bard, Tamren Jorbough.

Bersk briefly considered backtracking to collect the other third of his coin for taking care of the tainted fey, but it wasn't worth the two-day walk back. Not for ten silver. Hopefully, Tam had found better work ahead.

There was irony somewhere in the last days' mix of events—that Bersk was making even less now than he had when working for the Church. The hunter was a simple man, of simple tastes—especially when compared to the bard—but he had to eat, sleep, and keep his armor and equipment in proper order.

Thoughts of retiring like Manny the bartender, or Idina the hunter from Keld were far off, indeed. Bersk took his life and his work one day at a time. In that way, he wasn't much different from the poor fey, Aryvon—wandering aimlessly, more or less, hunting where he could, sleeping where he could. Both nursed lingering injuries—Bersk's maimed right hand ached beneath the glove.

The man, the hunter Kevril Bersk and the fey god Aryvon couldn't have been more different to look at them, but Bersk had understood the fey's pain and its desperation at the end.

To look into the eyes of a god was to look upon the truly alien. But even gods understood pain. Aryvon was more like a wounded beast than a man, and even men were dangerous when cornered.

Bersk was just glad that all Aryvon did was insult him—*who believes he is the son of Geof and Eisha.* Their kind seemed fond of that particular one and it wasn't the first time a fey had called the hunter such.

"Could've just called me a whoreson," Bersk muttered in between slashes of his sword. The hunter kept a steady pace as he bushwhacked through the brush and bramble to the hamlet Archimedes spied from above.

As much as the hunter tried to clear his mind, to focus on the rhythmically trek before him, he kept drifting back to the interaction with Aryvon.

The fey's corruption had run deep, deep enough that there was little left of the true god beneath. Not enough to save.

Everdeath had been a right bastard, that was for sure.

Kevril Bersk had spent the better part of a decade wading through the destruction left in the lich's wake. People always said that it was half the continent of Ozequn. Half was conservative, and even then, so little had escaped completely.

Even those cities that weren't destroyed lost scores of men to the war. The surviving civilizations were scared. Families torn asunder.

And one fey god maimed and left for death.

Sircius Everdeath had been an immortal and a sadist. Twisted by immortality.

Until he was abruptly and definitively stopped somewhere in the barren volcano flats to the North. Such an unexpected end that there was not enough struggle to mark where the bastard died. There were only the scattered remains of tens of his metal soldiers.

There was a part of Kevril that hoped Everdeath suffered and suffered painfully for all he had done, but there was something he liked better thinking that the lich was defeated swiftly and left without memorial at all.

And as the hunter bushwhacked through the forest, he thought it ironic that nature should recover so quickly while the world of men did not. But then, Everdeath hadn't been stopping to burn trees. Only settlements.

Bersk's mind wandered again to the bone shrine in the swamp of Keld—the shrine to Ariazi, the mother of demons. How it had hidden the village of Keld from Everdeath's rampage those twenty years ago.

And how Pater O'Malley confirmed that the number of demon shrines had been increasing as of late.

"That's what the Church is for," Bersk grumbled to himself as he walked. The Church and the Order of Kripishi—surely they would handle it.

Thoughts of Santa Anna came last and lingered long.

The last time Bersk had seen her, she was in the courtyard of the Septriones Church. They walked around the courtyard, side by side in the sun, Bersk with hands nervously clasped in front of him. Her wearing the red robes of the bishop, face all but hidden behind the wide hood. Looking back, he'd seen her face so few times in contrast to how often he'd thought of her: Her sharp features, green eyes and the dark curls of her hair. He'd seen her smile even less so, but it warmed him all the same, like the sun over a Winter's frost. And he'd thought of that smile often in his quiet moments.

Most memories of her were from that courtyard. Other bishops did not take kindly to a lowly Knight of the Order lingering in their sacred wing of the building.

Not that they talked conspiratorially—on the contrary. The time before that they talked about chapter fourteen of the Enchiridion, of the little city of Bronzehold, of Tam's exploits in said village, and then the weather. Rather mundane things compared to what other hunters and bishops talked about— they didn't talk about her work or his hunting.

But they lingered together, didn't they? She talked with a lowly Knight far longer than she would talk to another bishop, and Kev talked with her far longer than even Pater O'Malley. Only Tam and Archimedes had her beat.

There was that too: She called him Kev. Not often, but she did. About as often as she allowed herself to smile.

Bersk grumbled to himself as he bushwacked through the forest.

Here he was on the other side of the known world, daydreaming about a woman that couldn't be further from him. Anna was a bishop—*a saint*—of the Church; she was forbidden from almost everything material. Especially a lowly former Knight who had abandoned the Order—who was now on the other side of the world.

It was a dangerous, if not impossible thing, to hold two conflicting truths in oneself. Bersk was bound to the Gray

Queen and yet he would've given himself to Anna, who was bound to the Church. Like trying to concentrate on two spells at once—impossible.

And yet, technically, Bersk could do just that. But only because of *Twitch*—the sword of the Gray Queen.

Maybe that was why the skin of his right hand was wearing thin and was painful to the touch. Perhaps the Gray Queen was a jealous goddess.

Yet there was only one woman that Kevril Bersk thought of in his quiet moments, and it wasn't his goddess.

~

It was evening, and the sun was already falling when Bersk came across the small hamlet that Archimedes had seen from the sky. He stopped at the edge of the forest and the fields surrounding it, and breathed a sigh of relief.

The lodestone in his pocket vibrated. Bersk wrapped a hand around it and accepted the request.

A few moments later, Tamren Jorbough appeared twenty paces away.

Tam glanced around and smoothed the ruffles of his silk shirt and red sash. The bard looked as disheveled as Bersk felt. A small pack and a lute, painted deep green with white swirls, jostled on his back.

High above, Archimedes crowed in greeting.

"Ah, very good, Bersk." Then the bard turned to the sky and nodded to the circling raven. To Bersk he said, "I was hoping you weren't still on the road. Let's get ourselves a bath then."

Kevril smirked, then gestured to the bard's dirty clothes. "And where have you been?"

"Nothing so quaint as this, I assure you." Tam waved for them to walk as they talked. "A military encampment from Arkcaster. About two days Northeast of that last town.. Eh… You were still heading East, weren't you?"

Bersk nodded. "Got a little off track chasing a fey, but I should be back on course. What's this now about the Arkcaster military? Why are they venturing out?"

"It seems there's a land rush in the making. Arkcaster got word that the city of Zalledo is looking to expand. To take back *free land*, as they call it."

"They mean land that Everdeath burned to the ground."

Tam shrugged. "One in the same, to hear them talk. Truthfully, I'm surprised they held off as long as they did. At least they have a little respect for the dead."

Bersk glanced upward at Archimedes and beckoned the bird to come down. Moments later, the psychopomp flitted to his shoulder and cooed softly. Kevril stroked the raven's head.

Tam chuckled nervously. "Unpresuming little fellow."

Bersk said, "I doubt the cities waited as long as they did out of respect for the dead. They didn't have the manpower to spread their influence—not after Everdeath's rampage across the continent."

The bard smiled softly. "Yes, well that's true too. *Respect for the dead* sounds better. Sounds political."

"You're too kind to the nobles."

Tam stroked his long gray beard idly. "One shouldn't make a practice of biting the hand that feeds, Bersk. Those nobles pay well for entertainment. If I speak too freely, I'm liable to lose my reputation and have to resort to mercenary work."

Though Tam jested, there was a cold truth belying his words. One that neither man wanted to give breath to.

Archimedes ruffled its feathers, and Bersk changed the subject. "So, who did you find that has a monster problem?"

"Arkcaster. The military encampment."

Bersk slowed in the middle of the field. "You'll have to say that again, Tam. It sounded like you said the *military encampment has a monster problem?*"

Tam turned and nodded. "You heard right."

"And how big is this encampment?"

"Sixty or so soldiers. Horses, tents, some support personnel… What are you getting at, Bersk?"

Bersk and Archimedes shared a glance. "Must be a big problem."

Tam nodded. "You could say that. They found a hive. I'll tell you all about it. But first, this poet needs a bath."

~

The little hamlet that served as their layover was a quaint place, smaller even than the village of Keld from some days ago. It did, however, have a main thoroughfare wide enough for a wagon—this said more about the town than any other shops, smith, or merchant might have. And the people seemed no stranger to the occasional sellsword and traveler. As Bersk and Tam walked through the muddy streets, they garnered nothing more than a glance of acknowledgement and curious stare from children.

Some mercenaries preferred it when they could pass unnoticed through a town— they hid their armor and weapons so as not to draw suspicion. Pretend they were invisible or just another commoner.

Other mercenaries liked to wear gaudy armor and walk through the streets with the flair of a performer. These types paid the commoners no mind, unless they were tossing coin their way. These types liked to pretend that it was the commoners that were invisible.

Kevril Bersk liked it best when neither sellsword or commoner was a surprise to the other. Everyone going about their business as if they were all commoners—both equally invisible to each other.

The monster hunter couldn't say where that outlook came from—whether it was from his time as a Knight of the Order or his time on the streets—only that he couldn't remember living any other way.

The innkeeper didn't ask for Bersk's name, nor did he volunteer it. Nor did the guard they passed or the innkeeper's wife who brought them hot soup. Bersk only shared his name with those receiving his services—employers or targets. He spoke in nods and single words.

Yes, it was better that way. Here, he wasn't Kevril Bersk or even a former Knight of Kripishi. Here he was just another sellsword, just another shadow passing through. A ghost.

He didn't have the energy to be anything else.

But Tam, on the other hand, couldn't help but be charming. He was a bard and a poet, through and through. A word of thanks was never simply that; it was a smile and a flourish of the hand, never using one word when two or three might do.

Bersk admired this about his friend far more than it tired him.

~

The pair ate their soups in silence, Tam only once reminding Bersk that he would talk no more business until the bard had his bath.

A few silver got them the meager tidings that could be had. Two baths in a cramped room with no partition, and a single room to share. But it beat sleeping in the stables again.

When the baths were drawn, Tam was disrobed and in before the innkeeper had even shut the door. Bersk glanced away from Tam's thin nude frame, giving his friend at least some dignity.

Tam sank down into the water, closed his eyes, and sighed. The basins weren't much, but at least they were warm.

Kevril followed a moment later, sitting his armor and clothes to the side. Everything except the glove over his right hand.

Out of the corner of his eye, the sellsword noticed Tam peeking at his gloved hand.

Bersk sat down in the basin and winced at the warm water. "Don't go presuming on our friendship."

Tam scoffed. "You're put together all wrong. Besides, I would have *much* better taste."

Bersk laughed and sank as far down into the water as he could, which was only up to his ribs and his knees, but it was enough. He draped his arms over the sides.

"How is the hand, Bersk?"

Bersk stared at the wall in front of him with squinted eyes. There wasn't much point in being polite, he supposed. Kevril slipped the glove off his hand, revealing the thin-skinned and ghoulish appendage.

Tam stifled a gasp. "And you say O'Malley is taking care of it?" Bersk nodded and Tam added snarkily, "Movernus, man. You can put the glove back on."

The sellsword chuckled and draped his arm over the side, hidden from view. It felt good, if *unnatural*, to let the skin breathe.

"If we're talking business, then you should tell me about this hive problem." Bersk heard Tam's water slosh and could feel the bard looking sideways at him.

"Is it business to check in on my partner's health—dare I say, my friend's health?"

Bersk shook his head. "No, I suppose not. It hurts, the same as always. No worse. No better."

"What does O'Malley think?"

He wriggled his ghoulish fingers, but didn't answer for a moment. "He thinks it's getting worse."

"I'm inclined to believe him."

Kevril smirked. The bard and the preacher… The pair of them would agree on something like that.

"Bersk, couldn't you ask your mistress… The, uh, Gray Queen for aid, or something?"

Tam's voice lowered when he uttered her name. Bersk knew enough of his friend that he didn't lower his voice for secrecy's sake. No—Tam was genuinely afraid of invoking the name of a god whose works he had seen with his own eyes.

Bersk waved a dismissive, normal hand. "She's not the type of god you presume upon. She asks of me—not the other way around."

"Yes… That's how it ought to be, isn't it? The One God never sat right with you."

"This sounds like business, Tam."

"Nonsense. Just a little bathtub philosophy."

Kevril shook his head. "Hard to work for a god you don't believe in."

Tam's voice lowered. "Were all gods as brazen, it would be easier to believe in them."

At that, Bersk glanced back at his friend. "Certainly makes it easier to root out the bullshit. I've never doubted whether the Gray Queen or Ariazi or Ogren or Bondiotta existed.

"Now, what was this about a hive?"

Tam sighed. "Always to business… Arkcaster's company was crossing the plains to the North. They had to go around this cliffside… Well, come to find out there's a bloody hive in the cliffside *and* beneath the field they wanted to cross."

"They can't go around it?"

"Not without trekking miles out of their way. The cliffs stretch on for miles. Even climbing down the face is out of the question: It's several hundred feet down, and they don't know how far the hive stretches. Anyone climbing down is liable to get attacked."

"So why do they need me? There's nothing I can fight that a company of soldiers can't."

"You underestimate yourself, Bersk. They've already been stuck there for two weeks. They've resorted to hunting and foraging to supplement their rations. Even now, their hunting parties are being picked off and soldiers are being butchered in the night." Tam held up a single finger. "One well-trained man can succeed where an army fails."

Kevril smirked. "Jokes aside… What is it exactly that they want me to do?"

Tam glanced away nervously. "They want you to blow it up. They want to clear a safe passage for settlers."

Bersk squinted at his friend, taking it first as a joke. but Tam's face didn't change.

Tam added, "At first, their engineer thought that explosives placed deep enough would level the cliffside in question. But then someone suggested killing the queen, and said that would be enough to drive the creatures out."

Bersk lulled his head. "Either of those *might* be enough…"

"What is it?"

The monster hunter sighed. "I really wanted to wash my hands of this. Helping the common folk is one thing. Helping a city government is another."

It was Tam's turn to sigh and the bard grabbed the coarse sponge beside him.

"What?" Bersk asked.

Tam paused and pointed the sponge at him, as if challenging him to a duel. "You would be helping the commoners, Bersk. Safe passage wouldn't just be for the Arkcaster. It's for *people*. And forgive me, if I don't appreciate journeying days ahead of you into unfamiliar territory, searching for leads for you—only to have you about to wash your hands of the suggestion."

Kevril smirked. "I wouldn't want to presume on our partnership—*our friendship*. I just needed your writerly ways to see it clearly."

~

The sellsword and the bard finished bathing, washed their clothes, then retired for the evening to their room and the two small beds therein. Tam produced a bottle of wine from a far too small pocket of his bag and they shared stories of the last few days on the road.

As always, Tam had more stories than Bersk.

He told of singing with the barkeep in that little village and the reinforcements from Arkcaster that he'd rode along with the encampment.

When Bersk grew weary, he stepped outside to see the sun one last time before it dipped below the horizon. Then both men retired to their room. There was no window in the meager dwelling, so Archimedes would have to be content on the roof. One of the last things Bersk did was summon *Twitch* to his hand and wedge the hilt under the handle of the door.

It wasn't until both men were in their beds, and the stories had run their course, that Bersk said, "You never told me just what kind of hive the company found."

"Oh, I suppose I didn't. That's because they don't know."

Kevril propped himself up on his arm and turned to his friend. "But they found remains of victims. And they suspect there's a queen."

Tam nodded, covers pulled up under his beard. "I think that's another reason they need someone knowledgeable. They know about waging war against men, but it doesn't seem like they know a thing about fighting monsters."

"So no one saw anything?"

Tam shook his head. "It didn't sound like it. Scouting parties either came back unharmed or not at all. And no one saw what comes out at night and slinks into the camp." The bard shivered.

Bersk thought about making a joke to lighten the mood, but thought better of it. Clearly, the bard's time in the military camp had convinced him that they were in need of serious help.

The friends said goodnight and then Bersk rolled over on his side to sleep.

There was something else too that stifled the joke before he could voice it. Something didn't sit right with him about the scant description that Tam had given:

There weren't many man-eaters that nested in numbers that great—not in a hive big enough to stretch throughout a cliff-side and the surrounding hill. Even fewer creatures that were nocturnal and either small enough or bold enough to sneak into a guarded camp. Something wasn't right.

Either this poor brigade was dealing with a new species, an unprecedented gathering, or—the most logical answer—that they were really being attacked by two different types of creatures.

Tam was right—the soldiers needed his help. They might as well be commoners out there in the forest.

Bersk's mind turned in spite of his desperate want to sleep.

The world was just recovering from the campaign of Sircius Everdeath. Arkcaster and other places were just now sending soldiers out into the unknown. The only problem was that the monsters had already filled the empty wake that the lich had left behind.

~ ~ ~

Chapter 3
Ephemeral Journeys

KEVRIL BERSK AND Tamren Jorbough left the hamlet with the rising sun. Between Tam's knowledge of the camp's location and Archimedes's scouting, the pair took a direct route through the forest.

Contrary to popular wisdom, it was possible to travel safely through the forests and plains away from civilization. For all the talk of monsters reclaiming the wilds, it was possible to go a long time never seeing so much as a bear or a wolf, let alone a monster. All the normal camping precautions, such as securing their rations and keeping a fire lit at night, dissuaded monsters as well as lesser beasts. A group, especially one well-trained with weapons, had even less to worry about.

As the pair walked through the forest on the first day of their journey, the bard was trying to liken monsters to food.

"No, no, no. That's not what I'm saying, at all," Tam muttered. He walked beside Kevril, occasionally slowing to walk behind him when the brush got dense enough to bushwack through.

Bersk sighed. "Alright. Explain to me again how monsters are like food."

"Forget the forest and the bears and the monsters. Instead, imagine that we're walking through a city and we're trying different foods. If we're commoners, used to eating porridge and mash, then most anything is going to taste good to us. Or, commoners would be eaten by most anything—bear and humble wolf.

"But merchants, used to brushing shoulders with nobles, have more refined palettes. They need only worry about a well-prepared meal, one with flourish and garnish. These merchants are the travelers that know to secure their rations and to keep fires lit at night. They don't need to worry about wolves or bears, only the errant monster.

"A well-trained group… To continue the metaphor, a group of soldiers would be a group of nobles. Their palettes are so refined that no dessert or monster surprises them. They are prepared for anything! Even the most dastardly culinary monster!"

Tam's voice had reached a crescendo and even birds flitted away from the tree tops.

Bersk found himself laughing. "Tam, that's a truly ridiculous metaphor, *but* I think I take your meaning now."

"Are you sure? Because I can explain it again. I couldn't sleep through the night knowing that my wordsmithery missed its mark."

"So, what does that make us sellswords in your metaphor?"

Tam smirked with satisfaction. "I suppose we're royalty. Ready for anything and everything. Refined *and dangerous*."

"There's just one problem," Bersk added.

"And what might that be?"

"What about those meals fit for a king? Those singular dishes that make even royalty gasp."

Silence settled in between them, the implication being clear: What about those monsters too dangerous even for sellswords?

"Speaking of any lich in particular?" Tam snorted, as if he were afraid to chuckle at the joke.

Bersk nodded. "Did your father ever tell you that old ad age—something about not picking fights. No matter how big you were, there was always a bigger man out there."

"Yes, I believe he told me something of the sort."

Bersk said, "Well, it holds true. There is always a bigger man. Always someone better with a blade. For every fearsome sellsword, there was a monster out there even more cunning."

"What monsters do we have to worry about then?"

The hunter thought for a moment. "Not many, I suspect. The older and more powerful monsters that would give us trouble aren't the kind to wander around blindly. And they can usually be bluffed or reasoned with. Hags and liches rarely leave their lairs. Demons or fallen angels are always trouble. But what we really have to worry about are the true anomalies."

"Oh?"

"Something like the spirit trapped within the walls of St. Lillian Cathedral. The will of the demon queen, Ariazi. Somewhere out there are more monsters like Sircius Everdeath, whom half the continent couldn't stop. And there was *something else that stopped him*."

Tam mused, "There's always a better dessert, is that it?"

The hunter shrugged. "I suppose so."

"Then I guess it's good that desserts such as them are for singular purpose. They're not made for any old noble or royalty—certainly not for a commoner. They're made for the king or for the queen. Monsters like Sircius Everdeath don't just wander the countryside killing for sport. They have plots and schemes. So, the likes of us running into them are pretty slim, right? ...Bersk?"

"That's one way to look at it, but then again…"

"What's that?"

Bersk slowed and turned to his comrade as they walked. "Did I ever tell you that the Church found Sircius Everdeath's lair?"

Tam's eyes widened. "Gods, no. You didn't."

"I'll spare you the grisly details, but Everdeath had been experimenting on people. That's how he made his metal army. He took the souls of some poor bastards and used them to fuel his metal men.

"He was meticulous in his research. There were records going back for decades—for *decades*. He'd been scouring the acres around his lair, snatching people here and there, butchering them and using them for his research. They even found sigils from the Order of Kripishi. Even our own Knights weren't safe. You or I wouldn't have been either.

"That's my point, Tam. At one point, that monster *did* roam the countryside, taking commoners, nobles, and knights alike."

It was a long time before anyone broke the silence. The sound of Bersk hacking through the brush filled the void.

"We're still fine," Bersk offered. "Two capable men, well-trained in magic. We don't have much to worry about."

Tam chuckled nervously. "We'll just be wary of any strange creatures bearing sugary delights."

~

When the sun began to set, they stopped for the evening. Archimedes watched over the camp while Bersk dug a fire pit. Tam gathered nearby brush, set the bedrolls, and offered encouragement to his digging friend.

When they were done and the fire was lit, Bersk and Tam sat and shared foraged berries and dried deer. Both enjoyed a comfortable silence, one that comes from a long friendship.

Of all the things they could've talked about, *friendship* weighed on Kevril Bersk.

Thrice he glanced at the bard, and thrice thought better of it.

"Something on your mind, Bersk?" When his friend didn't reply, Tam added, "It mustn't be good for you to stay so quiet."

Bersk chuckled nervously. "You have a woman's intuition."

"Ah, a seer's gift for truth," Tam corrected.

"A poet's knack for hyperbole."

"...What is it, Bersk?"

The hunter sighed. There was no hiding it, nor sleeping on it if he tried.

"Have you given any more thought to what we talked about in Keld?"

Tam's eyes narrowed. "In Keld?"

"The little town that Everdeath forgot—the one with the brilgura."

Several moments later, realization hit the bard. "About walking away from our adventures? Giving up on the trade, as it were…"

Tam's stare drifted off across the fire, out into the darkness beyond.

For a moment, Bersk worried that Tam had forgotten about the conversation, and that Bersk had just brought his friend's attention back. Like calling attention to a magic trick and ruining it in the process.

"Yes, and no," Tam finally said. "One doesn't just walk away from a life like this, Bersk. Even when I venture into the city and woo the nobles for coin and pleasure… I still find myself thinking about the road. Not about the horror, mind you, but about the thrill. To live and to *see*—Gods, the sights we've seen. I may be a poet, but a warrior's heart beats in my chest.

"But… I fear that I am on the cusp of denying that calling. I don't truly know what to make of it. Call it old age or curmudgeonly, but I doubt—I doubt."

Bersk added, "There aren't many old sellswords. Maybe we should both reconsider our fates."

Tam smiled. "Maybe, indeed. But I doubt I would know how to live without nights like these. Without the wilderness, the camaraderie. Oh, to be a shallow poet crowding the streets and the taverns, singing about things they've never lived. Like a songbird who's never flown."

Bersk nudged his friend. "When you retire to a life of poetry and debauchery, I shall be sure to visit. Often."

Tam's face wrinkled in a bitter smirk. "In my tumultuous thoughts, I had hoped you'd retire, too. Every tavern needs a doorman, streets need guards. The gangs need ruffians."

"Could you imagine?" Bersk said.

The hunter and bard shared a quiet laugh. Of all the uncertain things in the world, the future was never promised.

"One day, perhaps," Bersk said when the moment had smoldered. "One day."

~ ~ ~

Chapter 4
The Brigade
Encampment

BERSK AND TAM bushwhacked through the morning and when the color was all but gone from the sky, Archimedes glimpsed the cliffs and then the army camp. The hunter saw everything through the raven's eyes. The forest thinned and gave way completely in some areas to plains. The Cliffs of Moor were just beyond that: Frost white, not particularly tall—only some hundred feet high—but they stretched from horizon to horizon.

Bersk now saw the predicament that Arkcaster's company was facing. The only way down without substantial climbing gear was the narrow slope alongside their camp. The very same slope that was blocked by the hive. They certainly were in a predicament.

The sun hung high overhead when Bersk and Tam finally made it to the camp. They approached from the South. Rather than going straight to the camp, Bersk used Archimedes to find the patrols along the outer edge.

The last thing the hunter wanted to do was look like they were sneaking up on a group of weary soldiers.

~

Archimedes perched in one of the trees at the edge of the forest, just above the wandering patrol. Bersk and Tam met them at the edge.

Both of the patrol were young men, wearing the standard brown uniform with orange trim, stained with flecks of mud or possibly blud.

"Who goes there?" one of them shouted.

Tam and Bersk stepped out from the brush with hands raised and absent weapons so as not to alarm them.

All the better, because both patrolmen were young and looked shaken. Both kept hands on the pommels of their swords.

"Sorry to alarm you, lads. It is I, Tamren Jorbough, the poet, returned to speak with your Captain Henring. I've brought the monster hunter I spoke of."

The stouter young man with a bit of fuzz for a mustache nodded to his companion and both relaxed. "We didn't expect you for another two days." He sighed heavily. "It doesn't matter. Captain Henring and the others will be pleased."

He looked Kevril Bersk up and down and nodded again. "I don't know much about monsters, but you look the part of a hunter, sir."

"Why lad, this here is Kevril Bersk, former Knight of the Order—"

"Bersk is fine," the hunter said, narrowing his eyes. "No need for formalities."

"All the same, sir—eh, Bersk," the soldier said. "We'll show you the way."

Bersk and Tam followed the soldiers, while Archimedes flew ahead to the camp.

~

They passed through another short section of forest before coming to the clearing proper. At the edge of it, lay the brigade encampment. A ditch was dug around the outskirts and then felled trees laid just beyond it. Five men stood guard at the entrance. Beyond them, a dozen large, white tents were set in rows.

A single flag waved just beyond the entrance—the crest of Arkcaster. A single red stripe on black..

The young, mustached soldier greeted the guard and called out for Captain Henring. Moments later, a dark-haired man with a twinkle in his eye and three bars on the shoulder of his uniform beckoned them to follow.

He introduced himself as Sergeant Weylan and asked for their names in turn. "It's a good thing you arrived early. The men are getting antsy."

Bersk said nothing, for as they walked through the camp, other soldiers stepped out from the flaps of the tents. Most were in various states of dress, brown uniforms half buttoned or in undershirts. All looked haggard, their faces twisted into glares of suspicion and sleep deprivation.

"Antsy is one way to put it," Bersk muttered as they followed the Sergeant. He silently bid Archimedes to watch from the trees outside camp; no need to bring any more suspicion upon them.

One of the tents they passed was patched and sewn. The remnants of several gashes and blood stains shown in the fabric.

"Gods," Tam whispered. "It's only been a few days. What happened?"

"The hive happened," Weylan replied. "And depending on who you ask, *other things*, too."

"Are you going to elaborate on that, Sergeant?" Bersk asked.

Weylan turned for only a moment. "It's best if you hear things from the captain. There's too much crosstalk as it is."

~

Sergeant Weylan stopped in front of the center tent, pulled back the flap, and announced their entry.

Inside were two more officers. Sergeant Weylan introduced them as Captain Henring and Second-in-Command Specialist Xandra. Captain Henring was a stout man wearing the orange sash of his commanding rank. A long scar ran down the right side of his face, marring his hairline and beardline.

"Welcome back, Tam," the Captain said. "You said you'd be quick, but I fear I underestimated you."

Beside him stood Specialist Xandra. She was lean, with short white hair and a piercing stare. When introduced, she merely nodded. Of all the soldiers Bersk had seen in camp—including the other two officers—Xandra didn't seem as if she'd lost an ounce of nerve.

Captain Henring bid them to sit at the small folding table in the center of the tent. They'd been examining the map in the center. Bersk and Tam took the two seats opposite them, then the pair of officers sat. Only Sergeant Weylan remained standing, in spite of the two other open chairs.

Everlit candles hung around the room, and two more sat on the table. It was hard to tell in the artificial lightning, but as the moment drew on, Bersk became convinced that the uniforms of the officers and the Captain were *immaculate*—laced with magic.

The Captain tapped his fingers on the table. "So, Kevril Bersk, your friend has quite a lot to say about your talents. You've… You've dealt with monsters like this before?"

Henring was looking down at the map while he spoke, the events of the last week clearly on his mind.

Bersk had sat down expecting the Captain to talk about Arkcaster or about their mission, but straight to business suited him just as well.

Bersk said, "So far, Captain, I've been told of a hive that stands between you and easy passage past the cliffs. And I've been told that you lost men on patrol and in camp in the middle of the night." The air hung heavy in the room, thick enough to cut. "I've dealt with many creatures, but I need more to go on."

Henring nodded to his Second, and Xandra slipped a small packet out from under the edge of the map. She unfolded the pages and laid them out atop the map. On each was a drawing of a different creature.

The first insect was labeled 'worker'. It was short and brown, the body clearly segmented. Its legs were long but folded high at the joint, so the body still lay close to the ground.

Xandra said, "These were the first creatures we encountered. They came above ground in groups of two or three, going over the side of the cliff to harvest some mineral or salt. At first, they were harmless."

She laid a second piece of paper on the table labeled 'guard', depicting an enormous insect. In contrast to the segments and thin legs of the first, its legs were thick like the trunk of a tree, the body a singular mass. The whole of it was covered in dark, interlocking plates like the plate armor of a well-outfitted soldier. In front of two small eyes sat three huge and blunted horns.

Xandra continued, "As we tried to approach the workers, several of these guards came above ground to protect them."

Bersk glanced curiously at the soldier. "What happened then? Were they provoked in any way?"

Xandra's face hardened. Beside her, Sergeant Weylan replied, "Some of our men were injured in a confrontation. We retreated. Our weapons weren't effective against the hardened shells of the guards."

The hunter put a hand on the table to pause her. "But were the insects provoked in any way?"

Captain Henring sighed and leaned in his chair. "Some of the boys may have thrown some rocks at the workers. Obviously, when the guards came, the men had to defend themselves."

Bersk rubbed the rough edge of the desk idly and nodded for Xandra to continue.

She laid the last page on the table, labeled 'image'. This depicted a long, slender insect set atop long legs that kept it off the ground. If drawn to scale, it would stand somewhere between the worker and the guard. Long antennae stood atop its head and long fins stretched from the antennae and ran down the length of its body. These fins were drawn to ebb and flow like the creature was underwater, and colored with greens, blues, and yellows.

Tam ceased stroking his beard and turned the page so that he could see it better. "You've written *mage* at the top. Why?"

"These we encountered last," Xandra said. "We had sent a scouting party to find the entrance to their hive. Some of the men took it upon themselves to venture too close. Instead of guards, these came for them. Hypnotized them. We nearly lost the whole scouting party."

Bersk asked, "They took them, didn't they?"

Captain Henring muttered, "The men walked right into the hive. Gods know what happened to them down there."

Xandra asked, "You've seen these creatures before?"

Bersk nodded carefully.

Tam looked up from the third page. "You mean they are *scions*, then? Mage, sorcerer, wizard, all those are words to denote someone who wields magic, but so far as I know, Terrans gain magic through study. There are beasts that have inherent magic. Scion is the word for it. They are born with their power. While they do not have the breadth of magic that a Terran can learn, it is usually more potent."

Xandra turned dismissively back to the hunter. "Do you know how to get rid of them?"

"It isn't that simple," Bersk replied.

"That's why you're here," the Captain replied.

Bersk glanced at Tam and then the three soldiers, meeting each of their eyes in turn. "If what you're telling me about the soldiers' interactions are true… Then something is wrong with the hive. These creatures are called Formicae. They're generally docile—to the point that you would need to kill many of their workers for them to care at all. They also stay completely be-low ground, and so it's rare for Terrans to notice them at all. Lastly, I've read some accounts of their hypnosis… but never on Terrans. It's a measure to help control the drones, coordi-nate attacks, or to turn away creatures. Formicae don't behave this way…"

Xandra and Weylan shared concerned looks.

Captain Henring said, "I don't need to tell you, Bersk, how important this is to Arkcaster. This is the only passable section down the cliffs. Even our small brigade can't get through with-out provoking the *Formicae*, as you said. There's no hope for a road through these parts if the insects are allowed to remain. No hope for settlement."

Bersk narrowed his eyes at the Captain. "I'm not in the business of extermination."

The Captain smirked, but returned his hard glance. "Nei-ther are we. But I know for certain that Arkcaster wants the valley, and they'll send more men to take it, if they have to… They'll send war machines and blasting powder. Unless you have a better idea."

"Heal them, maybe," Bersk replied. "A Formicae hive act-ing normally wouldn't bother travelers, not even under a busy road."

"What if you can't?" Xandra asked. "Could we *deal with them*?"

The hunter smirked. "If they can't be healed, then 'm afraid Arkcaster will have to wait. We don't have the numbers or the weapons to exterminate them." Bersk turned to the Captain. "Frankly, my way is the only option."

Captain Henring nodded slightly. "I'll trust your judgment, Mr. Bersk, but know this: The powers that rule Arkcaster will not look kindly at us returning empty-handed. For our sake and for the Formicae's sake, let's hope you're right."

Bersk said, "There's one more thing that we should talk about *privately*."

The Captain hesitated, before nodding to his Second and the Sergeant. Both Xandra and Weylan left silently, but with narrowed eyes. Tam looked sheepishly at the drawings on the table, and Bersk waited for several moments after the soldiers left.

"Your men have been attacked at night in camp?" Bersk asked.

"Butchered."

"How many attacks?"

"Twice in ten days we've been here. The first was shortly after the first attack by the guard insects. The second was two nights ago. Shortly after, your friend here stumbled upon our encampment."

"Captain Henring, there is something else attacking your men at night. The Formicae aren't active at night."

The Captain's eyes narrowed. "You said they were acting irrationally..."

"And they are. But after seeing your fortifications and how close the tents are together, there's no way the Formicae could get inside without your guards seeing."

Captain Henring stared off through the tent, considering the information. "What about flying insects?"

Bersk shook his head. "There's no Formicae that fly. You've seen all there is to see of them, except for the queen, and she is too large to move about."

The Captain stared off in silence, and the sound of Tam stroking his beard filled the tent. Bersk waited—Henring had the look of a man who hadn't given away all the details.

Finally, Captain Henring said, "The first night, Sergeant Weylan said he heard the flapping of wings just before the attack. It… It must be something else then if the bugs can't fly."

"What can you tell me about the bodies?"

Henring met his eyes, startled. "Butchered, I tell you. Chunks of flesh and muscle bitten clean off. Both men were dead from blood loss before they could say what happened. I've been doing this a long time, Mr. Bersk, and I've never seen anything like it."

Bersk leaned back in his chair. "I take it you buried them already?"

Henring nodded quickly.

"How many men on watch?"

"Two men each shift."

The hunter nodded. "Keep it that way for now. Tam and I will be extra eyes. With any luck, we'll catch it."

~ ~ ~

Chapter 5
The Cliffs

CAPTAIN HENRING, BERSK, and Tam concluded their meeting. There was still daylight to be had and Bersk wanted to see what the worker insects were harvesting on the cliffs. The captain called again for his two commanding officers and ordered that Sergeant Weylan and a trio of soldiers escort them to the cliffs.

As Bersk and Tam gathered out front of the captain's tent with the Sergeant and the Second, Bersk saw the contrast between the officer's uniforms and the enlisted soldiers. It had been a long time since Kevril had seen military ranks, but back then magical wears had been hard to come by, even for ranking officers. They were reserved for upper ranks—the Captain alone, for instance—or for the sellswords who partook in dangerous and lucrative work. Arkcaster was well off enough to afford magical armor for two more.

The Sergeant and the Second exchanged a soldier's salute and goodbye; though something struck Bersk as odd. It might've been their stares, how quick Weylan turned, or how long Xandra watched him walk away... but there was something unspoken between them—something more than military camaraderie.

Either way, Tam elbowed Bersk in the side and smirked, confirming Bersk's suspicions.

"Something going on there," Tam said.

"You're a dog," Bersk replied.

"But I'm not blind."

"Nor wrong." Bersk turned and continued toward the edge of the camp, Tam at his side. Meanwhile, Archimedes cawed and took to the sky. The psychopomp would scout ahead.

Most of the soldiers had returned to their tents. Of those that mulled around, fewer eyes were upon the sellsword and the bard as they walked.

Just when Bersk had thought they would walk out without incident, one young soldier stepped out in front of them. The sellsword and Bard stopped abruptly. Bersk held the man's gaze, puzzledly and half-expecting trouble.

The soldier brushed back blond hair, and wiped sleep from his squinted eyes, which glanced from Bersk to Tam. "Mr. Jorbough! Would you grace us with another song this evening?"

Bersk sighed, and Tam chuckled nervously, looking at his comrade.

"I'm sure you'll have time for your adoring fans," the hunter replied, clasping an arm around Tam's shoulder.

"I suppose..."

The soldier smiled at that and called back to the tents. "Do you hear that, Stanberry? Mr. Jorbough sounds like he might need some accompaniment!"

Try as the old bard might to keep his composure, his face went nearly as pale as the streaks in his beard.

Out from the tents came a tall wisp of a man. He stood proud, like a dark-haired sapling, wearing little more than long johns. "I've been practicing my scales, sir."

In the strange moment, Bersk felt a pit of concern in his gut for the stunned poet. He put a hand on the blond lad's shoulder and gently, but firmly, moved him aside. "All things in time. For now, it's business." Then Bersk ushered his comrade past them, to the edge of the camp.

Behind them, soldiers chuckled in laughter.

Bersk lowered his voice. "By the Queen… What was that about?"

But Tam didn't respond, not until they were past the guards and clear of the entrance.

The bard's voice was a trembling whisper. "The soldiers… When I was here last, they put that poor boy Stanberry up to sing with me. The lad's dreadful. *Absolutely* dreadful—"

"Mr. Jorbough speaks the truth," Sergeant Weylan said, approaching quickly. Weylan shook his head. When he was closer, he added quietly, "It's just a bit of fun between the soldiers. Something to take their mind off last week's events."

Bersk regarded the Sergeant warily. The soldier had good hearing—*exceptional* hearing.

Tam sighed and said, "It's just strange. Any other place he'd be laughed out of. Bersk, you don't understand. It's dreadful. I don't know how the men stand it."

Bersk turned to his friend. "Perhaps a spot of magic could help him next time, or at least ease everyone else's ears?"

The bard looked off thoughtfully. "I suppose it's worth a try."

Bersk turned back to the Sergeant. "Now, let's see to the cliffs."

~

Two low-ranked soldiers accompanied Bersk, Tam, and the Sergeant to the cliffs. Without being asked, the two men stayed a short distance behind to give them privacy.

Bersk waited until they were back in the forest and well away from the camp before striking up conversation, for he had two pressing questions for Weylan.

Bersk lowered his voice. "The Captain said you were on watch during the night of the first attack."

Sergeant Weylan nodded slightly.

"What happened that night?"

The soldier kept his eyes on the treeline as he recounted the events. "Nothing happened that night—not until the half moon was high in the sky. I heard the flapping of wings in the back of the camp. We were at the front. By the time we arrived... well, you heard the rest."

Tam rubbed his beard in contemplation.

"Did you see anything? Anything at all?" Bersk asked.

The Sergeant shook his head. "Just heard the wings one last time. I didn't get a good look at them."

"And where was the second guard that night?" Bersk asked.

"Right beside me." Weylan met his eyes for a moment before turning back to the path in front of them. "Why do you ask?"

"It's just that the Captain said nothing about the other guard hearing wings. Just you."

"I don't reckon he heard them," Weylan replied curtly.

Bersk lowered his voice to a whisper. "*You have very good hearing.*"

"What was that?" Tam asked, leaning closer to his comrade.

Bersk ignored the bard and saw a flicker of surprise on Weylan's face.

The hunter waved a dismissive hand. "I just said I found it curious that our culprit flew in and out of the camp so effectively."

Weylan shot Bersk a glare. "Guards patrol the camp at night now."

"Yet an attack still happened two days ago... Did they hear flying?"

"I'm not sure what you're getting at—"

"*Did they hear flying?*"

Weylan and the others stopped walking. And Bersk waited for the Sergeant to meet his eyes and offer an explanation. Tam was frozen, hand on his beard, eyes flitting between the two men.

The hunter leaned in and whispered, "I merely find it hard to understand how an experienced soldier, with magical armor and hearing such as yours, allows not one but two men to be attacked in the dead of night."

"That's enough, *ratcatcher.*" Weylan's eyes were narrowed. "Let's pretend that your questions are innocent and not accusatory. I was taken by surprise the first time, and asleep the second. And as for mine and Xandra's armor... It's minor magic, not the protective boons that your *kind* take for granted."

Bersk stared back, trying to read the man.

Weylan was lying about something. Bersk had half-a-mind to interrogate him with magic, but he doubted the Captain would condone such a thing. Most officers didn't entertain the thought of their comrades' disloyalty, and would even turn a blind eye to it—even when it was right in front of them.

"Let's pretend that we're both civilized men," Bersk replied, staring down the Sergeant. "Know that, for now, I need your trust and your sword…"

Weylan stared back, eyes cold. "And after?"

"That while I'm in this encampment, you shall be awake and on night watch."

The Sergeant said nothing. He merely turned and signaled for them to follow to the cliffs.

~

Before long, they came to the edge of the forest. From there, they could see the clearing and the cliffs. Off to the right lay a winding slope, almost as if a landslide had taken out part of the cliff face. It was a much more difficult path than Bersk had imagined—one barely befitting people, let alone carts and carriages.

Bersk gestured over to the rocky path. "That is the passage that the Captain and Arkcaster want to secure."

Weylan nodded. "The very same."

Tam spoke up beside them. "It's a little narrow for a main thoroughfare, don't you think?"

Weylan shrugged. "It's not my concern. That's between the Captain's intel and Arkcaster's orders—*there!*" The Sergeant lowered his voice and pointed toward the cliff.

To the left—the opposite direction of the slope—three worker bugs scurried out of the forest some fifty feet away.

Their brown, segmented bodies seemed to glide just above the ground on folded legs, and looked as if they'd just strolled off of Captain Henring's drawings.

It had been many years since Bersk had seen Formicae. Back then, he had ventured below ground with his seigneur— Pater O'Malley. He'd been struck by the single-mindedness of the creatures, and Bersk felt the same sentiment now. The workers scurried across the ground without any thought to their surroundings or predators. The guards were the same in their defense of the hive—fighting viciously and without pause for their own life or limb.

The scions though… they had been different. There had been an intelligence in their vibrant eyes. Something alien and unknowable.

Bersk watched the workers silently and intently for several minutes. A group of two or three would emerge from the forest, walk to the cliff's edge, and disappear over it. A few minutes later, they would walk back up, back to the forest, and be replaced a few minutes later with another group of workers.

Bersk couldn't see them carrying anything.

When the next batch of workers arrived, Bersk willed Archimedes to fly over the cliff's edge. The raven followed the insects thirty feet down the cliff's face, then turned into the warm updraft along the cliff's edge, allowing it to hover and watch.

Meanwhile, the hunter pretended to watch and wait from the treeline while he looked through Archimedes's eyes.

The workers were poised on the rocks, crunching at sections with their mandibles. At first, it was hard to distinguish exactly which colors the workers were interested in—for the wall was a mix of reds, oranges, browns and yellows—but soon the psychopomp saw for certain that the workers were eating the crumbling yellow sections.

Archimedes's eyes were even better than Bersk's own in some regards, but the hunter was going to go over the side of the cliff and look for himself—one, to verify what the raven had seen, and two, because Bersk was not going to explain that he had a tether to the bird. Random soldiers knowing he had a pet raven was one thing, knowing that he could see through its eyes was another.

"Stay here," the hunter whispered. "I'll be back in a moment." He waited for the next group of workers, then walked a dozen steps behind them.

Bersk stepped to the edge of the cliff and looked out over the landscape of the valley. It sprawled out to the horizon, a beautiful mix of greens—it was immediately apparent why Arkcaster wanted it.

Even though the hunter could choose to see through Archimedes's eyes at any time, there was something more real about seeing the sight for himself.

Then the hunter spoke the worlds, "*Vires et voluntatem*," to give him strength. Bersk slipped a small knife from his belt, climbed over the edge, and down the face of the cliff. The spell helped his hands and feet find purchase, and helped him fight the urge to look down past his feet.

The valley floor lay hundreds of feet below. Meanwhile, the raven glided in sweeping circles, riding the updraft.

Once Bersk had climbed down to the level of the workers, he clung close to the wall and waited.

When the workers turned to climb upward, the hunter made his move. He scurried across the rocky face to where they were digging. Whole crevices had been eaten away, leaving scars in the rock.

Bersk didn't need more than a moment. The smell of rotten eggs was overpowering. He used the knife to pry out a bit of the crumbling yellow rock, brought some to his nose and sniffed it. Then promptly coughed.

Sulfur. *Brimstone.* The smell that so often accompanied demons.

In the mortal plane, much of it was buried underground or already mixed with other compounds. But in the realm of the demons, it was plentiful.

It was also used to summon demons to the mortal plane.

Bersk shimmed back the way he came, away from the sulfur deposits before the next batch of workers came. There he hung, facing out toward the expanse of Ozequn, looking out over the landscape while his mind wandered elsewhere.

What use could the Formicae have for sulfur, and for so much of it?

The hunter climbed back up to the top, released the spell of strength, and then jogged over to Tam and the waiting soldiers.

~

Bersk slipped back into the cover of the treeline. Both the bard and the Sergeant gathered close to the hunter. The other two soldiers kept their eyes on the forest and the steady procession of worker insects.

"What did you find?" Tam asked.

"Sulfur. The bugs found a sulfur vein and are either eating it or harvesting it."

The Sergeant's face scrunched in confusion. "Is that normal?"

Bersk shook his head. "No. There's a chance it might be benign. Sometimes animals will seek out minerals or salt if their diet is poor, and perhaps the hive is much bigger than we originally thought. But sulfur has connotations…"

Sergeant Weylan stifled a laugh. "You can't be serious. Why, they're insects, for Lord's sake! If it were some occult crazies gathering sulfur, then I could understand your concern. They're insects, not demon summoners."

Bersk said plainly, "That doesn't erase the fact that they're harvesting sulfur in far greater quantities than they should be."

But the hunter trailed off. It seemed no amount of logic would erase the smug grin from the Sergeant's face.

Tam interjected, "I brought you the best hunter that Arkcaster could ask for, and you flagrantly disregard his explanations—"

Bersk smirked and held up a hand to stay his friend. "There are those that jest at the improbable and those who wait to laugh until the improbable has been ruled out."

Weylan grinned. "Well spoken, for a sellsword. How many tries did it take you to memorize that?"

The two men had stepped close to one another, staring each other in the eye.

"Have you ever seen a monster?" Bersk asked.

Sergeant Weylan's face flickered to a frown, confusion, and then back to that smug grin. "Is that some kind of threat, ratcatcher?"

Bersk shook his head. "I don't mean the worker bugs, a young vampire on the streets, or some poor lost fey… I mean the monsters that are so ancient and so removed from the world we know that you can't begin to comprehend their thoughts and motives." He gestured to the ground. "The queen of these Formicae—she's hundreds of years old. A single mind controlling hundreds or maybe even a thousand different bodies. She's suspended in the central chamber, like a paralyzed empress.

"Do you know that when a Formicae queen is desperate enough, she'll use her scions to capture and subjugate other species. Any normal Terran gets made a slave in war, no matter how bad the torture gets, you always have your thoughts. Any idea what that's like to be a slave in your own mind? To lose control of your body and not even have the salvation of dreaming of escape?

"You have men down there, Sergeant Weylan—slaves. They've seen monsters. Perhaps don't question the one man amongst you that's seen monsters *and killed them.*"

The words hung thick in the air and both men's eyes were narrowed at one another. At some point in the fervor, Bersk's gloved right hand left his side, as if to reach into the ether and summon *Twitch*—Weylan's hand had reached for his sword. Weapons all but drawn.

A crow sounded from the treetops. Bersk shifted his sight to the raven high above them. In the distance, trees swayed. Moments later, the cracks of saplings and the sound of a stampede swept through the forest.

"Sergeant!" one of the soldiers shouted.

Both Weylan and Bersk turned and stepped forward. Both the other soldiers instinctively stepped to the side to let the veterans in front. Meanwhile, Tam stepped further to the side and near the largest nearby tree.

"*Vires et voluntatem,*" Bersk said. His muscles once again swelled with strength and his chest swelled with confidence. With a flick of his wrist, *Twitch* appeared in his right hand.

He could have made a show of it, could have let the soldiers see just how easily the blade came to his hand, or show that he could concentrate on two spells at once. But Bersk would rather hide those things from the Sergeant—even if it made the upcoming battle harder.

Whatever was tearing through the underbrush was nearly upon them. Archimedes took to the sky and saw in earnest the massive swath cut through the forest.

Finally, the cracking and snapping of wood was upon them and through the treeline came two enormous guard insects of the Formicae. Their dappled plate armor shells seemed to glide toward them, plowing unperturbed through foliage and sending chunks of earth flying. They bellowed, blasting steam from between the thick plates, and shook the massive horns on their heads.

To the far right came the mumblers of incantation from the half-hidden bard. Meanwhile, Bersk strode forward to meet the guard beetle on the right—only vaguely aware that the Sergeant was walking beside him, matching the hunter's brazen steps.

As the first guard charged, Bersk slipped to the right and slashed at its legs. *Twitch* was a flash of blue, but the blade bounced harmlessly off the first and second legs, and only found purchase in the knee joint of the third—slashing clean through and severing the lower leg in a spurt of blue blood.

The beast spun around, barely slowed by the missing limb. Bersk ducked beneath the horns, slipping to the left of the guard and slashing quickly at its reinforced front leg—three times before *Twitch* cut completely through the knee joint.

Steam blasted from between the plates as it bellowed, and as it spun around to its left, Bersk stayed two steps ahead of it, slashing at the middle and back left legs in the same manner.

In a span of breaths, the guard beetle collapsed, only able to hobble with its two remaining legs.

The hunter backed away. In his dance with the monster, he'd wound up on the other side from the soldiers. So Bersk watched through Archimedes's eyes for a moment to see how the soldiers fared:

Sergeant Weylan motioned for the two soldiers to stay behind him, while he baited the attention of the other guard. The Sergeant backpedaled and circled around, dodging just out of reach of the horns. Even through Archimedes's distant gaze, Bersk recognized the footwork of a trained soldier. In the next breath, Weylan slipped the horns of the beetle—mirroring Bersk—and then slashed through the knee joints. The two young soldiers waited until the beast was on its last legs before lunging in to aid.

In those moments, Bersk also recognized a hex spell upon the beetle—likely courtesy of the bard.

Bersk absentmindedly stepped back from his own target, which thrashed both forcefully and impotently on the ground, and kept watching through the bird's eyes. When the other beast had been thoroughly crippled, Sergeant Weylan thrust his longsword between the creature's neck plates.

Moments later, Bersk did similarly; *Twitch's* blue blade disappeared into the beetle, sizzling quietly. Then the beast ceased struggling. Bersk dismissed his blade and stepped out from behind the carcass to check on his tentative allies.

Sergeant Weylan pulled out a rag and wiped his longsword before sheathing it. "Glad to see you're unscathed, sellsword."

Tam stepped out from behind the tree and breathed a sigh of relief. "Well, that was no brilgura, that I don't think I'd like to see those again either."

Weylan turned to Tam. "Thank you for your aid. A little unnecessary, but always welcome."

"Perhaps not necessary for some." Tam smirked and pointed behind Weylan to the two other soldiers, whose swords rattled nervously as they sheathed them. The bard shrugged and added, "A man does what he can."

Without pause, three more worker bugs marched along the clearing and over the edge of the cliff.

"We shouldn't linger," Bersk said.

The Sergeant nodded. "Back to camp then. The sun's already slacking in the sky."

"Not yet," the hunter replied. He walked over to the nearest dead guard, slipped the knife from his belt and pried open the thick mandibles of its mouth. Then with his left hand, he ran a finger just inside the mouth. When Bersk pulled his finger back, he found nothing but clear mucus. It smelled of earth and strangely sweet.

"That's lovely," Tam said through a wince.

Bersk stood and wiped the residue on his trousers. "No sulfur."

"Oh."

"That means they're not eating it," the hunter added. "They're using it for something else."

~ ~ ~

Chapter 6
First Glimpses of the Dark

SERGEANT WEYLAN WAS done talking. Whether it was the afternoon's events or the aftermath of battle, Bersk couldn't say. Either way, the Sergeant led the way back to camp with the other two soldiers, giving Bersk and Tam a moment to speak privately.

But not for a moment did Bersk imagine that the Sergeant couldn't hear their conversation. The hunter kept his eyes on the backs of the soldiers.

At least for a moment, in the cool air of the forest, tensions were assuaged

Tam walked beside him, still wearing a look of disbelief. "Gods, Bersk. What other reason could a hive of Formicae have for sulfur?"

The hunter just shook his head. "I don't know—really. Perhaps they found a demon burial chamber or an old summoning well."

"But you said the queen is smart and that she controls the drones. Why should she awaken a—"

"I said that the queen is smarter than we think. It's… It's difficult to speak of things being *intelligent*, when they're merely alien. Take a spider, for instance. Imagine a large spider that builds a brilliant web. The spider is good at web building, but is it smart? That is harder to say. The queen might not *understand* what she's doing."

Tam stroked his beard and mulled this over. "When you put it like that… Frankly, I'm not sure what's more terrifying—coming across a giant spider or a demon."

Bersk chuckled. "I can see it now on the world's worst stage show."

Tam scrunched his face and changed his voice to that of a hawker. "Step right up, step right up. What will it be sir, madam—door number one or door number two? The poor sods!"

As the chuckles faded, Bersk felt Tam nudge his arm. Tam gestured to the soldiers up ahead and mouthed 'sergeant'.

Bersk shook his head and tapped his ear.

Whatever the bard wanted to talk about, it was going to have to wait until nightfall.

Tam cleared his throat obnoxiously. "What about the Formicae?"

Bersk shook his head. "I won't know what they're up to without going into the hive."

Tam's eyes widened. "I beg your pardon. It sounded for a moment like you said you were going to go down in there with the guards and scion bugs, and Gods know what else."

The hunter shrugged. "I didn't say you had to come with me."

"Oh, thank Movernus for that."

~

The conversation faded as they neared the encampment. The guards stepped aside, their eyes falling to the sellsword and bard. Again, soldiers stepped out of the rows of white tents to watch them as they passed, but none spoke. Not even when Archimedes fluttered down to the outer rows.

Bersk and Tam walked past them, following Weylan to the Captain's tent. Inside, a smile flashed across Captain Henring's scarred face.

"So, found anything useful?" Henring gestured to the chairs.

Second-in-Command Specialist Xandra stepped in a moment later and stood patiently beside Sergeant Weylan.

"I won't be staying," Bersk said. "Your Formicae are harvesting sulfur from the cliffs—far more than could be coincidental. I need to figure out why."

Henring's face wrinkled in thought and his eyes flitted to the sellsword and to some point beyond the white walls of the tent.

"Very good, for now. You'll need to go down there, won't you?"

Bersk nodded. "I'm going there shortly. The Formicae are dormant at night. I can be in and out before night completely sets." The hunter glanced at Tam, who stood intently at the map upon the desk. "I trust Tamren Jorbough can put his songs to good use in the meantime."

Captain Henring smirked. "That will do just fine, Mr. Jorbough. As for you, Mr. Bersk, Specialist Xandra will accompany you into the hive."

"That won't be necessary—"

"I didn't ask," Captain Henring added. "Non-negotiable."

Bersk stared at the Captain. The man leaned on the table, both hands clasped together—exuding both calmness and authority. In that moment, Bersk silently wished he had made better use of his truth spell.

Bersk looked to Xandra, who returned his harsh gaze.

The hunter sighed. "I have magic that will conceal me."

Xandra smirked. "So do I."

"She's a specialist for a reason," Captain Henring said plainly. "She'll be a second set of eyes to confirm what you find."

Bersk nodded quickly, not taking his eyes off the soldier.

He already didn't trust Sergeant Weylan, and there was clearly *something* between the Sergeant and the Specialist. If Bersk's hunch was right and there was something nefarious about Sergeant Weylan, then Specialist Xandra was likely in on it as well.

Going into a Formicae hive with a possible enemy was not how Bersk wanted to spend the evening.

The captain cleared his throat, bringing the sellsword's attention back to him. "Mr. Bersk, I want you to make the missing men a priority." Stoic concern hung on his face.

"I'll do what I can. Finding and stopping whatever is causing the Formicae'S erratic behavior comes first. If I need to, I'll go back another night for them."

Henring nodded, appeased.

Bersk turned to his new partner and said, "The sun's already low. Are you ready?"

Xandra nodded, her expression as unreadable as steel.

Tam met his eyes with concern, no doubt reading the unspoken tension on his friend's face.

"I suppose you can handle yourselves down there," the bard replied, reluctantly.

Bersk nodded, trying to assuage his friend's concern. "I'll be back before nightfall."

~

The hunter and the specialist walked quickly past the soldiers, who were still gathered in front of their tents. Bersk had no idea of what they had heard of the conversation or what the Captain would share with them. But where before the soldiers watched in silence, now the hunter and specialist left murmurs in their wake. Neither of them paid any mind to the soldiers' concern.

They entered the forest, and as they walked, Bersk turned over in his head just how little he trusted the specialist and the sergeant. Sergeant Weylan had superior hearing and was proficient enough with a blade to stand down a charging guard beetle. Then there was the fact that Weylan was the only soldier to hear the wings of whatever creature attacked the camp on the first night… And then heard nothing the second night.

Sergeant Weylan was no regular mortal Terran. Bersk had seen too many strange and wondrous creatures that *looked human* to be convinced otherwise. Furthermore, the sergeant had taken offense to the accusation and was hiding his abilities from the other soldiers.

And Weylan and Xandra were close. Perhaps even conspiratorially close.

Of the creatures that looked human, about half of them fed on humans. The elven city of Novissimé had ways of screening and keeping out such creatures, and some human kingdoms had begun using types of magic detection to flush out some as well. So that left lower human societies, small cities, remote villages or military outposts where these creatures could live and feed unbeknownst to people.

Weylan and Xandra could be two such creatures… And if that was true, then the Formicae were the least of Bersk's worries. The soldiers had been very careful and cunning to survive in a place like Arkcaster (even with the blood dens) and especially if they had lived through the events of Sircius Everdeath's campaign across the continent.

Bersk bid Archimedes to follow above the treetops. Before this development, Bersk had half a mind to bring Archimedes into the hive. But now the hunter was torn between descending into the hive with the psychopomp or leaving the bird above ground. Below, Archimedes could be a second set of eyes and an accomplice to violence, but then Xandra might learn just what his familiar was capable of. If he left Archimedes, then he would have one more trick up his sleeve should violence break out in the camp… but then he would be below ground with a woman he didn't trust.

The one consolation was that once they were underground together, Bersk had a vision spell that would help him see in the dark and protect him from the hypnotizing power of the scions—

It would also narrow down what manner of being Specialist Xandra was.

Bersk grit his teeth in frustration; he needed a stealth spell to get him through the caverns unseen. If he were to use both that *and* the spell of sight, then Xandra would know he could concentrate on two spells at once—another significant advantage that he wasn't willing to relinquish.

Beyond the treeline, the sun was bleeding orange in the sky. The hunter and the specialist walked abreast through the darkening forest.

Xandra was staring at him. "Are you always so suspicious of soldiers?"

Bersk glanced at her in acknowledgement, but returned his gaze to the treeline. "Who said I was suspicious of anyone?"

"You didn't have to. Weylan is an easy enough man to read. When you returned from the cliffs it was written all over his face."

"That's a lot to discern from a man's face."

Xandra shrugged. "I thought at first it might be jealousy, but you don't strike me as the womanizing type. Or that he might have been frustrated, but then there weren't any wounds or even scuffs on you or the other soldiers. Then I think that you had questioned him about the men that died in the night… And now I see it written on your face."

The hunter sighed. "Are you trying to change my mind about your lover?" Bersk turned to watch her reaction through both his and Archimedes's eyes.

Xandra smiled quickly, her cheeks turning pink. "He's not *just* that. And you never answered my question: Are you always so suspicious of soldiers?"

"It's not because you're soldiers. It's because he lied to me. Because he hides his powers." Bersk judged her eyes, but Xandra didn't blink at the mention of powers. "Do you trust him?"

"With my life," Xandra replied, white hair blowing in the breeze.

Bersk nodded and turned back to the treeline.

"What if you're mistaken?" she asked calmly. "Do you think he is happy that those men died? Or perhaps he knew where your accusations might lead?"

The hunter sighed. "Are we close to the entrance?"

"Only a few hundred feet to the edge of the treeline, then another hundred more to the entrance. That much closer to earning your coin and being rid of us."

For the first time, Bersk heard irritation in Xandra's otherwise level voice.

"For what it's worth, I hope I'm wrong."

Xandra waved a dismissive hand. "You sellswords are all the same. Swoop in, do a job, take the money, leave others to live with the mess."

Bersk ignored the insult. A moment later they came to the edge of the treeline. In the distance, laid a giant crevice in the ground—the entrance to the Formicae hive.

"When we go in," Xandra said. "Just do your job. I'll be right behind you."

~

The pair stood on the edge of the treeline as the sunset was turning red. Archimedes perched several trees away, glancing between its master and the hole in the earth.

Still intent on revealing as few of his tricks as possible, Bersk offered to cast a single spell on both of them.

"*Hidden in plain sight* can get us through undetected," he offered.

Xandra nodded. For a moment, her stare was so intense, Bersk worried she could read his thoughts.

She said, "And I can cast *darkvision* on both of us."

The two nodded tentatively.

With both sellsword and specialist relying on one another's spells, one would be less likely to stab the other in the back. It was a suitable compromise in his eyes, especially since Xandra wanted him to go first.

Bersk scanned the clearing at the cliff's edge for any sign of workers.

"What's your plan, Mr. Bersk?"

"When worker Formicae gather food, they bring it back and deposit it in central rooms for the hive to eat. They'll be doing the same with sulfur. With any luck there's still a shift coming back that we can follow." He just hoped they hadn't gotten to the hive too late to follow the insects—otherwise he would need either a guiding spell or to bring Archimedes down there with him.

Xandra asked, "Just how deep into the hive are we going?"

Bersk shrugged. "Food is usually stored near the eggs and larva. There are small pockets all throughout the hive. But sulfur… it depends on what they're using it for. They could lead us anywhere down there."

A look of uncertainty flashed across Xandra's face, but the specialist said nothing.

"Stay by my side and remember the path we take," Bersk said sternly, meeting her eyes. "There will be countless twists and turns. If we get separated—"

"Don't worry. You won't leave my sight."

After a few minutes, a trio of worker insects came walking back from the cliffs. Bersk breathed a sigh of relief. Xandra and Bersk cast their spells for vision and silence. Then Bersk led Xandra across the short clearing to the hive entrance.

Green grass gave way to a hole ten feet in diameter. With magically enhanced sight, the mix of dirt and rocks was colored in shades of gray. Bersk could follow the gentle slope as it curled around itself. He waved for Xandra to follow, and the pair started down the tunnel and into the hive.

Hidden in plain sight was a potent spell for incursions like this. Neither he nor Xandra would leave behind scent or footsteps, nor sound of breath or tremor of their steps.

The only thing it did not hide was the sight of them, but then most of the Formicae didn't rely on sight. Only the scions and the queen bothered with such a sense when they all lived in total darkness.

Even if Bersk wanted to be completely concealed, *True invisibility* was an incredibly difficult spell to cast and to control—other mages might spend a whole career mastering one such a high-level spell.

The pair stalked into the hive as quiet as ghosts and followed the worker bugs along the descending tunnel. The tunnel curved in a wide arch and before long, their steady procession brought them to the first junction.

The steady tap—tap—tap of the worker's legs echoed through each of the tunnels. Bersk glanced down each tunnel as the workers continued straight, but saw nothing beyond the gray curving walls.

Two worker bugs appeared around the bend, coming the opposite direction. Both sets continued, like carriages doomed to run into each other.

At the last moment, the oncoming insects changed their course slightly, arcing up the left side of the tunnel. The workers that Bersk and Xandra were following did the same on the right side of the wall. The hunter and specialist followed them as best they could on the slope of the tunnel wall.

Bersk held his breath even though he didn't need to, and didn't breathe again until the oncoming workers had disappeared behind them.

The sellsword glanced behind him and saw Xandra breathe a similar sigh of relief.

They passed several more junctions, each with three or four branching paths. If one merely looked in the direction, it might've seemed nonsensical, but each twist and turn by the workers took them further downward. Bersk committed the turns to memory, while also plotting a mental map—

They were hundreds of feet below ground, practically plunging into the earth in the fastest direction possible.

The ground and the air in the tunnels grew cool, and in spite of it, Bersk was beginning to sweat. At first, he had merely been curious at what was causing the Formicae to behave strangely and venture above ground, but dread began to mount in the sellsword.

What could the Formicae be doing with all that sulfur?

What had they found down there?

Bersk steeled himself, pushing aside the dread and the curiosity, and focused on the task at hand.

~

Deeper and deeper they went.

Twice more Bersk looked behind him in the gray silence, wondering if the specialist was still with him—twice Xandra met his gaze reassuredly.

Bersk's unease about her company was all but forgotten. They were much too far down. Formicae hives were known to sprawl.

Bersk shook his head. He'd counted two-dozen junctions. This was much too far.

A warm breeze blew through the tunnel, and as they followed the worker bugs through the next junction, the tunnel quickly grew sweltering. Bersk's shirt was heavy with sweat.

Finally, the end of the tunnel glowed with a soft, shimmering red light. Bersk and Xandra followed the workers to the end.

The tunnel blossomed into a cavern and Kevril Bersk stopped at the edge, mouth hanging open as he took in the sight. The cavern stretched some hundreds of feet across. Above them, Bersk saw the cavern tapering to a jagged point some equally immense measure above them.

The contour of the rocky walls was broken by great smooth cylinders that wrapped nearly around the whole passage. As Bersk's eyes adjusted to the newfound color, he realized with astonishment that these strange smooth sections were rib bones of some ancient gargantuan beast, and that the entire cavern seemed as if it was carved inside its fossilized stomach.

Magic lingered here. A residue of power that hung as thick as mist. It felt as if the air itself was electric, like a storm bottled and brought into the earth.

In his time wandering the realm, he had felt other residual magic such as this. Sometimes it can linger in the wake of a god, or in the grave of a powerful being, sometimes even in the wake of a mad wizard—like the volcano flats to the North where Sircius Everdeath met his end.

Bersk had never been to the Flats, but he had walked the graves of gods and never felt a power like that which lingered in this cavern.

The hunter finally looked down, his gaze following the ribs and rock wall some two hundred feet below them. There the immense space ended in a twisting mass of jagged bone, some amalgamation of creature that Bersk couldn't begin to guess at. In the center, a fleshy mass pulsed with life.

But it was impossible to tell just what was going on below without getting closer.

Bersk turned his gaze to follow the worker bugs down the slope. There was a semblance of a path down the edges of the cavern, one that looked just passable by Terrans.

The sellsword motioned for Xandra to follow and the pair started down the slope, half crawling and half sliding.

It wasn't until they were halfway down that Bersk fully comprehended what he was seeing: The bones of the ancient giant that lined the wall continued down the entire way, ending somewhere down in the ground—as if the whole cavern was merely one segment of a titanic serpent.

But the bones at the center of the cavern floor weren't the remains of a single creature—they were a mass of rock and bone, the whole of it radiating and rippling with molten heat.

And in the center of it all—the spots of flesh—was the queen.

O'Malley had once shown Bersk pictures of the Formicae queen. Queens were huge and towering, with a body that might reach across the cavern, sitting atop legs that could reach fifty feet.

But here, the queen was contorted through arches of bone and rock, her legs mangled and lifeless around the outer rim of the ground. Trapped and bound.

The worker bugs that Bersk and Xandra had followed walked all the way up to the queen's maw, forced themselves inside her and deposited stomachs full of sulfur—the yellow sludge pooled in front of the queen's face. The cavern shook with what Bersk could only assume was agony.

Bersk saw the twisted bone and stone anew. Just as residual magic could be left behind, others tried to harness that magic. This was an altar. An altar to the mother of all demons built inside the carcass of a dead god.

The Formicae had unwittingly stumbled upon the site—something buried so deep it was unfathomably old. The queen was a sacrifice.

The sellsword didn't have time to feel pity because as the worker bugs walked past him and Xandra, a new insect appeared from behind the altar.

A set of long fins ran the length of its body, flowing as if it were underwater. The fins shimmered from green to blue and yellow and back again. Bersk recognized what should have been a scion… but the creature was easily thirty feet long—four times longer than normal. Instead of thin, wispy legs, it stood upon giant spears which clacked violently against the stone floor as it walked. Its face, too, had been warped—the eye sockets were deep and sunken, its mandibles enlarged to the size of meat cleavers.

The giant scion walked around the altar and stopped in front of the queen. It raised its antennae, unfurling its fins to their full width. The colors on them changed to a swirling hue of blood and sunset.

The pitiful rumbling of the queen ceased completely.

Bersk felt a hand on his shoulder. Specialist Xandra was beside him, eyes narrowed, and hand on her sword.

Bersk shook his head. They were only there to scout.

Xandra nodded reluctantly.

The pair turned to scale the slope and begin the long trek up through the tunnels, but both sellsword and specialist froze.

A human soldier walked slowly toward them, face blank, eyes vacant. His mouth and chin were coated with yellow sludge. All down the front of his armor was caked with the grime. He walked in a stupor, somehow navigating the precarious slope with only a slight misstep, despite not looking down.

The pair watched in horror as he walked toward them. When he passed, they turned to follow—

And found the scion staring at them. It stood tall, with its antennae and fins held high and wide. Ready to hypnotize them!

Bersk turned away. But when he looked at Xandra, her eyes were wide, her face frozen. The shimmering red light of the scion already dancing across her face. She was paralyzed.

As the sellsword contemplated his options, he was vaguely aware that the red light had grown harsh in the room as his *darkvision* faded—as Xandra no longer able to maintain her spell.

The vacant, entranced soldier disappeared somewhere beyond the scion and the altar.

"*Vires et voluntatem.*" Bersk uttered the words of strength, followed quickly by one more—

"*Omni-videns ordinem.*" The spell of *all-seeing order*. Bersk's eyes became filled—blotted out—with the same blue glow as his sword, *Twitch*. Magic dripped from his eyes like glowing, weeping tears.

As Bersk looked upon Xandra's face, the shimmering reds were replaced with a haze of bright blue. The whole of the cavern was bathed in the same magical hue.

In that moment—for that was all he had—he saw a glimpse of Xandra's true self: She was human in shape, but otherworldly strength flowed through her veins, hardened her bones, and burned in her muscles. Her hard confidence was born from this hidden power.

He turned and looked upon the possessed scion with the protection of the Gray Queen. The flowing iridescent fins were filtered to harmless blue. The scion rose up to its full height, its slender neck reaching nearly twenty feet in the air. It stared back, the mix of strange and evil intelligence embodied within it, realizing that Bersk was immune to its power. Its mandibles chattered before finally opening wide in a screeching bellow.

The scion charged up the slope, its spear-tipped legs stabbing the rocks, fins tucked along its side, and its body undulating like a viper.

Bersk turned, scooped the still mesmerized Xandra over his left shoulder, and sprinted. He bounded up the slope with magical strength, his feet finding purchase on the rocks. Clacks echoed behind him—the scion's steps!

He was nearly at the tunnel entrance when he felt the stabs of the scion shaking the ground beneath his feet.

Bersk leapt, soaring up and across the last remnants of the slope. He spun and conjured *Twitch* to his right hand, and found the scion nearly upon them—limb raised in the air and poised to strike.

The beast brought down its spear-tipped leg, thrusting it toward them. Still airborne, Bersk lashed out with his sword. In a flash of brilliant blue, Twitch severed the end of the scion's leg. The beast stumbled and screamed.

Bersk landed in the tunnel, ready for the scion, but the beast paused on the slope. Its mandibles chattered with uncertainty.

"Put me down," Xandra said warily from his shoulder.

"Can you stand?" Bersk asked, not taking his glowing eyes off the beast.

"I'll be fine in a moment." She stood and glanced at Bersk while keeping the scion out of her view. "Do you have a spell for speed?"

Bersk traced a sigil with his left hand. "*Astar na gaoithe*," he said, casting the spell on both of them. The *speed of the wind*.

The scion backed away down the slope, its steps erratic. Then the beast's body began to shake with intermittent pulses. Though the sound was too low for Terrans to hear, the loose rocks on the ground began to vibrate in time with the beast.

The scion was calling for the hive to wake up.

"Time to go," Bersk said.

Xandra cast *darkvision* on herself again. Then hunter and specialist turned and ran with otherworldly speed, leaving the scion, the Formicae queen, and the altar behind.

~

Kevril Bersk's eyes burned with the power of the Gray Queen, filtering the tunnel in bright blue light. Seeing with the power of his goddess felt like a dream—all the more poignant because of his speed. The rocky walls of the Formicae tunnels blurred and, for a moment, the hunter felt like he was flying.

But the rumbling of the hive brought him back to the moment.

They sprinted past junction after junction as the ground began to rumble as if the whole hive stirred for their blood.

Bersk focused on counting the junctions as they ran, Xandra just behind him, nearly stepping on his heels. They passed the first seven junctions before the bugs arrived.

At the next junction, the massive horns of a guard beetle emerged from the hall. As it turned to face them, the hunter and specialist hugged the left side of the tunnel, running across the nearly vertical surface with their otherworldly speed. They were around the bend before the beetle could turn to follow.

Twice more, they narrowly avoided the hulking bodies of the guards—all the while without slowing their frantic pace.

They passed half a dozen more junctions before the insects could make it to the main thoroughfare. They were two junctions from the entrance when the scions came for them.

These scions were expected—just as Bersk remembered and just as the captain's drawings. They were no bigger than the worker bugs, and much more slender. And so far as the hunter could remember, they were harmless other than their hypnotizing visage.

But they poured into the tunnel in droves, clambering over one another to wave their iridescent fins and trap the escaping Terrans.

"Keep your eyes on my heels!" Bersk shouted.

"Do not worry about me, sellsword," Xandra called back.

There was nothing to do but go through them.

The magic speed within him flowed not just to his legs and senses, but also through his sword arm. *Twitch* was a blur of fearsome speed, carving through scion after scion—the gore of it all filtered blue by his sight. Without slowing or pausing, the hunter barreled through the flood of Formicae like the bow of a dreadnaught through rough seas.

Behind him—thankfully—he heard the intermittent slash of steel as Xandra followed in his wake.

Moments later, the pair burst out of the tunnel and into the field. Without pausing, they raced to the treeline.

~ ~ ~

Chapter 7
Moonlight Admissions

TAMREN JORBOUGH STROLLED idly through the military encampment. He had fully expected the men to requisition him for a song, but it had now been nearly an hour since Bersk had left, the sun was setting, and no such requests had been made.

Which was all the same to Tam because he had no desire to repeat his duets with the lad, Stanberry. Poor tone-deaf Stanberry.

But now Tam had the opposite problem: *Boredom*. What was a bard to do?

Tam chuckled to himself. Normally, he might've found his way to the bar or to a maiden, but he was working, after all. Even if his job was marginally easier than delving into an underground hive full of vicious insects, a man had to have standards.

Besides, he wasn't particularly fond of being off alone with a woman when soldiers had gone missing—plucked right out from camp.

So, he strolled. And pondered.

In another life he might've been a military man. Gods knew *that* would've made mother proud. It also, quite possibly, would've made him dead, seeing as how his hometown had been in the direct path of Sircius Everdeath's crusade.

But as Tam strolled around the encampment, watching soldiers playing cards and dice, and sharing stories around the fire, he saw the appeal of camaraderie. Brothers and sisters forged in bond of service. It was why he had stayed with Bersk so long… and also why he longed to leave the adventures behind and start a *normal* life, for lack of a better word.

The bard walked through between the rows of tall white tents.

Tam chuckled again and muttered to himself, "Yes, that would make mother happy."

Tam turned the next row and froze—Stanberry was several rows away and walking with a lute. The sight of lanky, dark haired, long john wearing man struck the bard like a tone deaf nightmare. A hollow pit formed in his stomach, and he lunged back the way he came.

Up until that point, Tam thought he'd prepared himself to sing again. He was wrong.

He peered around the tent and saw Stanberry talking with another soldier. Stanberry hadn't seen him. Tam still had a chance to escape.

Quickly, he glanced either way, weighing his options. He took off a moment later, walking quickly, panic fueling him. He zig-zagged through the rows of tents, putting distance between himself and the lad.

The bulk of the soldiers must have been out mingling, because most of the tents seemed completely empty. All the better, Tam thought—no chance of a soldier yelling out for a song and calling the lad down upon him.

Or so Tam thought until he turned a white corner and found Sergeant Weylan standing at the other end of the row. He stood with arms crossed and eyes glaring. In the twilight, the sergeant seemed as wide as the row.

"Oh, uh, good evening to you," Tam stammered. He turned to run, but Sergeant Weylan appeared at the end of the row—blocking his escape. Tam glanced between where the sergeant had been and where he was. It was an impossible feat of movement.

A part of Tam wanted to yell, but the rest of him was paralyzed with silence.

So he ran the other direction, back the way he came. For a moment, he heard nothing but his own panicked breathing and his own feet pounding the ground.

Tam turned the corner and looked back—

Sergeant Weylan was a row behind him, staring.

Tam didn't stop. He zig-zagged back the way he came. Each time, he saw the figure of Weylan standing at the end of the row, following him.

Tam turned the next corner, and rough hands grabbed his collar. Tam winced and shut his eyes. "Please—don't!"

"Here he is!" said a gruff voice.

Tam squinted and found himself at the hands of a group of soldiers. Stanberry being one of them.

The men released him. Stanberry brushed off and straightened Tam's collar.

"The men would like a song, sir," Stanberry said, while the other men chuckled.

Gods above, Tam never thought he'd be glad to see Stanberry.

Tam looked quickly around, but saw no sign of the sergeant anymore. "I, uh…" Tam breathed deep and forced a smile. "I suppose I can do with that, lad."

"Are you sure, Mr. Jorbough?" asked a voice from behind—a voice that made Tam's blood run cold. Sergeant Weylan walked slowly around to stand behind Stanberry. "You look as if you've seen a ghost."

Tam held Weylan's gaze, and said as calmly as he could, "I gave myself a fright back there. Nothing more."

Stanberry wrapped an arm around the bard and ushered him through the tents and toward the center of camp. "I can't tell you how much it means to me to sing with you again…"

Tam half-listened and nodded haphazardly in agreement with the lad. *Whatever he wanted*, Tam thought. It would be safer to be singing with Stanberry than trying to hide from him.

~ ~ ~

SANTA ANNA WATCHED the fields pass through her carriage window. In the distance, jagged spires loomed, marking the citystate of Mortecen.

Santa Anna leaned her head against the warm glass. She could just make out the sprawling gardens that marked the edge of the Septriones Church. They were lit by hundreds of lanterns so that they looked like a glimmering sea. She smiled—a small and fleeting gesture. The gardens were beautiful despite her current predicament, and Anna resolved to enjoy them even if she only passed through the center.

It was strange to be home so soon—to have crossed half the known world in some two weeks compared to the two months it had taken her originally. Portal gates had cut down the journey significantly.

She adjusted her hands on her lap. They had begun to ache these last two days of travel. Despite her pleading, the guards had refused to remove the metal antimagic gloves or even unbind her hands.

Several times Santa Anna grew irritated at the pain and inconvenience, and had to remind herself that the guards were just following orders. She imagined it as practice for her upcoming disposition—refining her patience to deal with the Church's hierarchy.

Her seigneur had been fond of the saying: *The wheels of bureaucracy are slow to turn, and quick to crush the singular beneath them.* She was most likely to be cast aside or made into a scapegoat.

For those reasons, Anna had spent the last few days rehearsing what she would say—mulling over ways to present it so that it both seemed as dire as it was and yet not like outlandish ravings. By the end of the first day, Anna had decided to forgo *softening* of the news, and merely state what she had found before the elders in all its horror and glory:

The end times had come early—those fated scriptures that the Church both lamented and longed for.

"Only when night has fallen, do we know how few candles we have left," she said quietly. A passage from the *Imum Libra Terminus*—the *End of Balance*.

One of the guards sitting opposite her wrinkled his face in question. The other continued sleeping.

Santa Anna said nothing more. She watched the moonlit countryside roll by through the carriage window, waiting to see the gardens.

~ ~ ~

KEVRIL BERSK AND Specialist Xandra breathed heavily in the treeline. They looked back tentatively at the entrance to the hive, waiting to see if the Formicae swarm would follow them.

As the moments dragged on, they breathed easier.

"I don't think they'll follow," Bersk said. "They're too focused on whatever dark ritual they're trying to complete."

He released the spell of speed. Dull burn filled his muscles and his lungs—evidence of their long ascent through the tunnels and of holding his spells for so long.

Though the moon was out and a thick crescent in the sky, he still saw the forest and the open field in a haze of bright blue from his goddess's spell. Bersk turned to regard Xandra. She had a hand on her sword and looked back at him warily. As the moment lingered, he saw the rest of her—not just her inhuman strength and body.

Her magical armor wasn't for protection, but similar to Tamren Jorbough's: Made to hide stains. With his magic sight, Bersk saw the front of her armor stained with blood that glistened bright blue.

And her face… her skull jawbone hid slender fangs. The retractable teeth of a vampyre. One of the few creatures that can pass for human.

"Tell me what you see, Mr. Bersk." And when he didn't answer right away, she shouted, "Tell me what you see!"

"Everything."

It felt as if the world was still between them. All was silent, save for Bersk's beating heart and steady breath. The tentative truce they had underground felt as if it stood on a blade's edge.

Xandra was poised to fight. Even without magic, she would be a formidable opponent. Young vampyres were dangerous—mature vampyres with combat experience and magic were forces to be reckoned with. Even with his own magic, even conjuring *Twitch* to his hand at the speed of thought, and with Archimedes waiting quietly in the tree above them, the battle would be ferocious.

Yet, in spite of her gifts, Bersk saw Xandra clearly, and she was afraid.

Bersk let go of his goddess's magic. The electric blue glow of power that covered his eyes and dripped from them like wax vanished. The color faded to the gray and shadow of a half-moon night.

"Down in the hive, did you know? Did you see me then?"

"I wasn't sure."

"But you suspected."

Bersk nodded.

"Are you going to kill me?" she asked, muscles tensing.

"That depends." Bersk tried to keep still and keep his voice level. "Tell me what happened in the camp."

"Why bring me back… if you were just going to—"

"Because I saw the way you looked at that soldier down there. You were shocked—distraught. It wasn't the surprised look of a monster. It was the look of an officer contemplating how to rescue her soldier.

"What happened in the camp, Xandra? What happened to the two men in the middle of the night?"

Xandra's face softened and her feet shuffled uneasily, but her hand didn't leave the hilt of her sword. "His name was Paulson. The other two were Mhiko and Rolande."

She breathed a heavy sigh before continuing. "I stayed hidden for decades. Feeding little by little."

"I know of the feeding dens," Bersk said. "I assume Arkcaster has them."

Xandra added hesitantly, "There are others that are sympathetic to our plight. It was easy to hide in the cities. But it's been almost three weeks since we set out here. I fed on animals, but it's not the same as human blood. But you know that, don't you, hunter?"

"I'm a hunter. It doesn't matter whether my target is human, elven, or something else—I hunt *monsters*. I have no quarrel with feeding dens— no matter what creatures partake. So, I ask again, Xandra. What happened in the camp? Do you care about some of the soldiers and not others?"

For the first time, Xandra stood tall and took her hand off her sword. "Mhiko was a friend. He let us feed on him. It was hard, but we all managed that way.

"But then we came here, above the hive. Above that god's damn altar! We knew something wasn't right. The animals weren't satisfying our thirst, but only for a moment. We lost control that night… Then in our shame, we mangled his body to make it look like something else had attacked him.

"Rolande… He was a prick. He didn't deserve death, but we had no alternative. We are running out of time, hunter."

Xandra stood defiantly, in spite of the admission and that she had admitted Weylan's truth, as well.

She asked, "What are you going to do now? Are you going to kill me? I owe you my life, but I won't just let you take mine."

Bersk stared at Specialist Xandra—at the vampyre laid bare. And he felt weary from the weight of it all and from the struggle through the hive.

Finally, he said, "We have more pressing things to deal with. Whatever the Formicae are doing with the altar can't be allowed to continue. I don't know if there's any hope for the hive… or for your men down there. But if there's any chance of saving them, I need your help tomorrow night.

"So for now, your secret and your crime are safe. But heed my words, you and yours need to control your thirsts another night or I will have no choice. Can you do that?"

After a moment, Xandra nodded, and the tentative truce continued… at least for their walk back to camp.

~

The hunter and the specialist walked through the dark forest, navigating by the faint light of the moon, and came upon the encampment to find a most disconcerting sound emanating from it. The sound of the bard's lute, accompanied by a duo both sultry and ghastly.

Bersk winced in disapproval.

Meanwhile, Xandra chuckled. "It seems like your partner has been entertaining the camp."

"*That* is not the voice I remember."

"No, that is the lad, Stanberry," she said, wiping her eyes. "Your man is a saint."

Bersk flashed back to meeting the soldier before they left the encampment—the look of pale horror that had overcome Tam's face.

The pair rounded the walls of the camp, all the while the hunter's eye and neck twitched from the sound. They nodded to the two soldiers guarding the entrance and walked in. All the while, Bersk felt a sense of apprehension—of dread—at moving closer and closer to the sound. As if he were walking back into the depths of the hive and toward the altar again.

Archimedes perched on one of the nearby tents and even the raven seemed to twitch in agitation.

The brigade of soldiers were gathered on the ground in their plain clothes. The origin of the sound sat on a crate in the center—Tamren Jorbough playing his lute, and the thin lad Stanberry.

Kevril Bersk had seen the bard work wonders with song. Not only did the bard have the gift of voice, he was intuitive when accompanying another singer—matching their volume and guiding their pitch. Bersk had seen singers grow in skill just from a few duets with Tam, as if he were teaching them while singing with them.

It was akin to a master painter guiding the arm of their pupil, not painting for them, but enhancing their own innate style. Or even sculptors—the bard helping them unearth the pupil's voice from the rough block of stone.

But the scene and the song going on before him…

It was like a master trying to teach a toddler to paint. There was no hope in guiding the boy's brush to the canvas when he was content to sling paint upon the walls.

To the lad's credit, he knew most of the song. Every now and then his voice would lull during a verse and then his voice would explode when he remembered the end of the verse—as if he were trying to make up for lost volume.

And Stanberry knew all the blasted chorus.

"Carolaine,
Darling Carolain,
Never known such a bless and bane."

As the song neared its end, Bersk did manage to smile in spite of the assault on his ears. There was something innocent about the scene that softened the pitch—something about the magic of song bringing them together, about the soldiers finding respite, and even Stanberry's sheer joy of slinging paint across the walls. Or even the smile peeking through Tam's face at the epicenter of it all.

And as the song ended, Tam caught sight of Bersk and Xandra and his eyes lit up with surprise.

Tam stood and gestured to Stanberry. "Give it up for your boy—the second coming of Bellasandra LIesl, everyone! I'm afraid you'll have to excuse me." Then Tam handed Stanberry his lute and shuffled away through the crowd, leaving the poor lad to stay wide-eyed at the instrument.

The bard came up to the waiting hunter and specialist. "You're a sight for sore eyes, both of you."

Bersk glanced between the bard and Stanberry. The latter of which was plucking randomly at the strings while the crowd uneasily called for an encore.

"Are you sure your lute will be alright?" Bersk asked.

Tam nodded quickly, wincing at a note behind him. "Oh yes. She's a sturdy girl."

~

Xandra led them to the Captain's tent, where both Henring and Sergeant were waiting at the table. Both men stood to greet them, and Sergeant Weylan's eyes lingered on Specialist Xandra.

"What did you find?" Captain Henring asked. He glanced at both Bersk and Xandra, but the specialist deferred to Bersk.

"We found out why the hive is acting strangely," Bersk said. "There's a demonic altar buried deep underground. It's influencing the hive. Twisting them. Brainwashing them."

The Captain's gaze fell to the table and he breathed slowly. "Why in the Lord's name would they get in league with demons?"

Bersk replied. "The hive is expansive. They likely stumbled on it while they were digging. Once they unearthed it, the altar started influencing them. I've seen it myself. Sometimes just being near it is enough for the altar to mess with a mind. But it's not just that, the whole area could be influenced by it: Trees, animals, any other creatures with demonic heritage, or Terrans with fragile minds."

While Captain Henring contemplated the gravity of the development, Sergeant Weylan met the hunter's eyes.

Weylan asked, "So you're saying that our nighttime attacks could be caused by a creature under the influence of the altar?"

Bersk nodded, staring at the Sergeant. "Which means it could happen again. Tonight, I suggest extra guards on patrol. We all survive one more night, and we can put a stop to this tomorrow."

Weylan's eyes flitted between Bersk and Xandra, the unspoken agreement passing between them. Meanwhile, Tam stroked his beard and glanced between the group.

Captain Henring sighed and leaned heavy on the table. "What do you suggest, Mr. Bersk?"

Henring looked as if he already knew that there wouldn't be an easy end to it.

Bersk said, "Our main objective is to either destroy the altar or disable it. I can destroy it, but I won't have enough time—not without the entire hive coming after me. And we don't have an army or enough mages to fight the Formicae. Instead of destroying it, we can collapse the hive and bury the altar—once again laying it dormant beneath the earth."

Henring said, "We have blasting powder. Ten sacks of it. That should do it."

"Good," Bersk said. "There's just one problem. Your men are still down there."

"You found them?" Weylan asked, perking up a little.

Xandra shook her head. "We found one man. He was brainwashed. We didn't see anyone else."

Bersk added. "They're likely alive… but finding them is another story."

At that, Tam ceased stroking his beard. "Do you have something of theirs? Their personal effects or clothing?" When the soldiers nodded, Tam continued, "I have a tracking spell. But I could only lead you to one man at a time."

Bersk felt a lump in his throat at the thought of Tam going underground with them, but before he could protest, the Captain spoke up.

"Merciful luck," Captain Henring said.

Specialist Xandra spoke up, "I'll take Sergeant Weylan and a small team with us to accompany Mr. Bersk."

Bersk nodded. "I'll need the best. We'll go tomorrow night when the hive has settled down."

~

The captain dismissed them, and Bersk and Tam retired to a tent that had been left for them. Two cots and two thin blankets sat inside.

Meanwhile, Archimedes watched as Xandra and Weylan retired to their own tent. Bersk silently bid the bird to keep a close eye on them. If there was any danger to be had that night, it would be from the two vampyres.

The two comrades sat on their respective cots, facing one another.

Bersk said, "I wish you hadn't suggested going underground."

"I can't leave good men behind, Bersk. Not when there's something that I could do."

"Can't you use the spell above ground? Cast it on one of the soldiers, then let them go down while you concentrate on it."

Tam shook his head. "You're thinking of that time in Canterbury, and I could barely do that through a few walls of wood and stone. The hive's much too deep."

The bard was right, of course.

Bersk shook his head. "It's not going to be fun down there. Not after today."

"I didn't think bugs were one to hold grudges."

"Not usually, but they're not in control. Usually a Formicae queen runs the hive. The scions transmit commands to the workers and the guard beetles. The altar, or whatever is trying to come through the altar, has taken control of a scion. They're sacrificing the queen."

Tam shrugged, trying to hide his unease. "I guess we'll just have to be quick, then. Get in and get out before the buggers even know we're there."

Both men shared a smirk. Bersk didn't like it, but there was no point in trying to backtrack now.

Tam asked, "Did you find out about, you know." He gestured in the direction of Xandra and Weylan's tent.

Bersk nodded, then conjured *Twitch* to his hand in a silent flash of blue. He scrawled the word 'vampyre' on the ground. Then he scuffed the word out with his boot and dismissed the blade.

"That explains it," Tam said, rubbing his beard. "The man's an ass."

Bersk winced with a stifled laugh. "He can probably hear you."

Tam's eyes went wide for a moment, before he stuck his tongue out in mockery. "Can't hear that."

"Thanks for not helping me on the field, by the way," Bersk said in jest. "You helped Weylan but not me."

"You seemed like you were sandbagging! Which led me to believe you were doing that for a reason and had everything under control."

Bersk waved a dismissive hand. "I was gauging him, but I think he was doing the same to me as well." The hunter lowered his voice. "Both the officers are very good. *They're not young.*"

It took Tam a moment before the bard grasped his meaning—that they were not young vampyres. The officers were older, competent, and powerful. The bard nodded slowly at that.

"So… is, uh, everything alright then?" Tam asked.

"For now. They understand that there are more pressing concerns. Frankly, I need their help if there's any hope of getting the captured soldiers out or of bringing the hive down. I can't do it alone, not even with a bard's help."

"Well, we bards aren't all powerful. Also, thank you for leaving me behind. It wasn't so bad entertaining the camp. Bless that lad Stanberry. The boy sings like a deaf priest walking across tacks, but he does know quite a few songs. Or rather, he knows *most of the words* in those songs."

Bersk smiled. "Your patience has grown with your talent."

"Hah! And here I thought I'd plateaued." When the levity of the moment passed, Tam asked, "What about daylight tomorrow?"

The hunter sighed. "I suppose I should see Pater O'Malley."

"About the altar?"

Bersk nodded.

"That's two altars in a month," Tam said. "That's a record, isn't it?"

Bersk nodded again. His thoughts were far away. "You should've seen the map in O'Malley's study, Tam. The damn thing was covered in markers. A little flag for each sighting and cleansing of an altar. The Mother of Demons has been busy."

"What do you think it means?" Tam asked in a conspiratorial whisper.

"I don't know," the hunter replied in earnest.

"Is that the only reason you want to go back?"

Bersk met the bard's eyes. His friend knew him too well. "Of course not."

"They haven't heard from her yet?"

Bersk shook his head. Saint Anna—a bishop on the run. Over the last week, Bersk had been losing sleep over her. And O'Malley was probably the only contact in the Church that would share details about her trial…

It was just a matter of time before the Church found her.

"She'll be okay, Bersk," the bard said, his voice soft. "They'll figure out she's innocent and soon it will all be behind her."

Bersk grunted noncommittally.

Whatever happened and was going to happen between Santa Anna and the Church, it was out of his hands. That was what wore on the hunter the most.

Chapter 8
Crimson and Blood

SLEEP CAME FITFULLY to Kevril Bersk that night. The times he did drift off to sleep were short and punctuated by dreams of walking with Santa Anna in the courtyard of Septriones Church. Of course, her face was hidden by the red robes of service. He couldn't remember what they talked about, only that someone would call for her, and Anna would take off running across the courtyard, disappearing in a swirl of red. Each time, all he could think was that he longed to see her face again.

But his sleep wasn't entirely the fault of Santa Anna.

Archimedes perched above the tents, keeping lookout. Three tents away, occasional shadows moved behind the white fabric: The two vampyres, Specialist Xandra and Sergeant Weylan.

And they didn't sleep *at all* throughout the night. Whatever it was that vampyres did, they were careful and quiet.

So long as they stayed that way.

~

As soon as the sun began to rise, Bersk woke Tam and bid him farewell for the moment. To which the bard grumbled, nodded, and went back to sleep.

Bersk thumbed the lodestone in his pocket. A few minutes later, the lodestone grew warm in his hand—the signal that Pater O'Malley accepted his request to meet.

"*Ut dominus originis.*"

~

A moment later, Bersk appeared in Pater O'Malley's study beneath the Septriones Church as quickly and silently as the times he summoned *Twitch*. The Pater, Bersk's former seigneur, stood behind his ashwood desk. Everlit candles flickered around the room, highlighting the ancient tomes and harsh stone that surrounded them.

O'Malley offered a quick bow. "Kevril, to what do I owe your presence?"

"You look tired, Pater." Bersk sat in one of the heavy chairs and felt the chill underground air finally settle on his skin.

The priest nodded quickly and sat. "No rest for the weary."

For a moment, Bersk had all but forgotten what he was there to say as he was beset by memories of working for the Church—the many times he had sat across from his seigneur and discussed history and tactics and all other manner of things…

The hunter shook his head and came back to the moment. "We found another altar."

O'Malley said nothing at first. The wiry priest merely leaned back in his chair. The holy book—the Enchiridion—lay splayed out on the table before him.

Behind him hung the map of the known world: The twin continents of Eadruin and Ozequn, and the Frozen Isles to the south. And adorning it were hundreds of pins and tassels marking the location and dates of discoveries of altars to the mother of demons.

Bersk found it poetic in a way—that one might be safe down here beneath the stone and wards of the Church, even clutching the Enchiridion… But did that mean anything if demons continued to claw their way to the material plane?

O'Malley rubbed his forehead. "You're not that far from… Keld, was it? That last altar."

"Just a few days Northeast. It was buried underground."

"Was?"

"A military brigade stumbled upon a Formicae hive acting strangely. I went underground and found an old altar beneath the main chamber. One of the scions must have stumbled on it. It was mutated and under the altar's control. The Formicae are feeding the queen sulfur and meaning to sacrifice her."

"Did you take care of it yet?"

"Not yet. I'm taking a small team underground with me. They have enough blasting powder to collapse the hive and bury it again."

O'Malley nodded slightly. "That should take care of it, but how in the Lord's name did you get regular soldiers to volunteer?"

The hunter smirked. "Two of them are… *enhanced*." Telling O'Malley that they were vampyres would only complicate things.

At that, the priest smiled and then frowned immediately after. "They're not demon-blooded, are they, Kevril? Because taking them down to an altar is about the dumbest thing you could do. I'm surprised they agreed to it. They must know the risk they're taking by going closer to it."

Bersk waved a dismissive hand. "The altar is hundreds of feet below ground, and I'm not taking anyone down to the altar."

"But they're already affected by it, aren't they?" O'Malley's voice was cold—that of a teacher scolding a student.

Bersk narrowed his eyes. "There are men trapped down there. Mesmerized by the scions. I need their help to rescue them."

"Again, I'm surprised they agreed to it. That's all. Not like monsters to self-sacrifice."

"They're not all monsters," Bersk replied. But as soon as the words left his lips he regretted it. There was no point in having that debate again.

O'Malley scoffed in agreement.

The Church saw most everything in absolutes—in black and white. Monsters were to be eliminated. There was no room in human society for them.

It might have been easy to think that way when someone lived their life in service to the Church and the Lord, when they lived their entire life in black and white. Believe in the Lord and none other. Read this book, not that one. Donate money. Eat this, not that.

Kevril Bersk had left the Church and the Order of Kripishi because he had wandered the world, living amongst commoners, nobles, and tradesmen alike. He knew firsthand that the world was a shade of gray. There were other books, other beliefs, other gods.

Pater O'Malley had retreated to study and seclusion, to the texts that could only pretend to describe the world.

But something else seemed to be gnawing at the priest. Something else driving a wedge between and stoking their agitation.

"You seem even more on edge than usual," Bersk said. "Did the Church stick you with a new disciple or revise a passage again?"

The former seigneur stared back, eyes softening. "I wish it were only that."

When O'Malley didn't answer right away, Bersk jested, "Quit with the dramatics. There's no secrets between us."

"They found Santa Anna."

The words cast a silence between them, like bright light followed by harsh shadows. Bersk felt the breath leave his chest.

"When?"

"Earlier this morning."

"Gods, man, is she alright? What has she said?"

O'Malley held up a hand to stay him. "They found her yesterday morning. She's still being brought back. She's due to arrive in half-a-day's time. Apparently she was all the way South of the Frozen Isles, so it's taking a mix of boats, roads, and runes to make the journey. She's cooperating with extradition.

"That's all I know," the priest added. "She hasn't spoken a word to anyone since they found her."

Bersk slumped back in the chair. All he could picture was Santa Anna's face hidden by the veil of her crimson robes.

"Have they… Have they said anything about their plans or a trial?"

O'Malley shook his head. "The bishops are being tight-lipped. They still haven't said what she's been accused of."

"Well, what do *you* think?"

"Honestly… I'm trying not to dwell on it. You need to have faith in these things. Especially when they're out of our hands."

Kevril Bersk was a man who had walked the realm, fought alongside and against mortal and demigod, alike. He knew better than most other men that there were things in this world beyond his control.

Even Bersk's life was no longer his own, sworn to the service of the Gray Queen.

And he refused to let Santa Anna's fate be one of those things.

Bersk stood quickly. "You will let me know when she's arrived?"

O'Malley raised an eyebrow. "I'm worried about her too, Kevril. But the bishops will not let you or anyone else see her. That's protocol. It will be another thing after the questioning and after the trial—if it comes to that." The priest shook his head incredulously. "You're lucky you're even allowed to come see me, you know!"

Bersk was only partially listening. He was already thinking of how he could see Santa Anna—protocols be damned.

He said slyly, "When this Formicae business is taken care of, I'll likely need to come back for salve."

O'Malley rolled his eyes, then pointed a finger at Bersk. "So help me… Don't go mucking this up. Or they'll have both our heads…"

But Bersk had already pulled out the lodestone and thumbed a circle on the face of it. "*Ad locum meum.*"

~

When Bersk appeared in the tent, he did so silently and without fanfare.

Tam was sitting up on his cot and rubbing his eyes at the time.

When the bard finally opened his eyes, he recoiled back and nearly fell off the cot. "Damn it, Bersk. We need to put a bell on you or something."

Bersk mumbled in agreement, hearing absolutely nothing other than the general surprise from the bard. He was busy plotting and scheming how to get close to the holding cells of the Church.

Tam looked at him quizzically. "So we'll get you a bell then?"

The hunter nodded absently.

Tam grumbled. "Something not right about scaring a man so soundly, then ignoring him." When Bersk still didn't respond, Tam shouted, "Bersk!"

At that, Bersk startled and then sat down on his own cot. "Sorry about that."

Tam wore concern on his face. "What happened at the god-botherers's place?"

"They found Santa Anna."

"Oh shit. Is… Is that a good thing or a bad thing?"

"Not sure. She's not back yet, so O'Malley didn't have a lot to say on the matter."

"Ah, so that explains your inner turmoil."

Bersk finally glanced at his friend. "Is it that obvious?"

Tam chuckled and said sarcastically, "Only to the discerning eye."

"I need to see her, Tam."

His friend's face softened. "Do you really think that's the wisest course of action? Haven't you both been trying to keep your affections a secret? If you go to her in your current state, you'll only confirm their suspicions."

Bersk winced. "I know. I know… I was thinking about how to see her secretly."

The bard scoffed. "Secretly? In the most warded place in all the realm? You've really lost your lodestone, haven't you?"

"Maybe," was all Bersk replied.

Tam groaned in frustration.

~

Kevril Bersk and Tamren Jorbough ate brunch with the soldiers. Dried beans and berries. Afterward, Tam and Stanberry played a set to help pass the day.

Bersk appeared to watch from the back of the crowd. In reality, he was looking through the eyes of Archimedes. The raven had followed Specialist Xandra and Sergeant Weylan through their afternoon patrol of the forest.

Bersk had watched them chase and catch a doe. They were currently hunched over it, both taking turns draining blood from deep wounds in its neck. They sucked hungrily—desperately—at the deer. Things were getting dire for them.

All they had to do was make it one more night. One more night and the altar would be buried again. Their thirst *should* abate enough for them to tolerate it, for them to journey back to Arkcaster without incident. Back to the ready supply of blood dens.

O'Malley and the Church wouldn't approve of the blood dens, or of Bersk working with vampyres. Most hunters wouldn't either, Bersk supposed, but both were necessary evils. The blood dens kept vampires from feeding on the unsuspecting and from getting desperate and draining victims dry. Everybody lived that way.

The Church's zero tolerance policy for vampyres and monsters assumed that one could, in fact, get rid of all the monsters. They believed this regardless of how long and impossible such a task was, or how much war and suffering it would necessitate. Again, seeing the world in black and white.

What they wouldn't admit was that there was always another monster. Demons and their ilk existed on another plane of existence, and would *always* try to cross over. There was no getting rid of them. There was no end to it.

They wanted a black and white answer to a gray problem.

No, it was better this way. Placate the monsters. *Civilize them*, as some called it. Or learn to live with them.

Or *manage the damage*, as Bersk was fond of saying.

Either way, more Terrans lived this way.

But even as Archimedes watched the grisly scene from the treeline, Kevril Bersk wasn't really there either. He was busy thinking about how he would see Santa Anna, and preferably do so without the Church knowing.

The Septriones Church was warded against most magic—so much so that certain spells would not work on the premises. This included ones that would be useful in Bersk's current predicament: Teleportation spells, for instance, were completely negated without a lodestone. And lodestones were keyed to specific rooms of the Church.

Most illusion spells were negated as well. There was no tip-toeing around with *hidden in plain sight* or even a higher-powered invisibility spell. Enchantment and divination spells were also negated unless in confessional booths or in the *interrogation wings*, as they were politely called.

Other spell bans were more obvious, like necromancy. Archimedes's shapeshifting or merging powers wouldn't work either.

But of the spells that could work, most were combat or defense oriented. In other words, nothing useful for snooping around.

As Bersk mused over his options, the music played, and the afternoon dragged on, he realized with growing disheartenment that there wasn't a way for him to see Santa Anna—not in secret.

For a desperate moment, Bersk even considered asking the Gray Queen for assistance. But he just as quickly reconsidered. There were deities that spoke with mortals and those that didn't mind mortals asking things of them—even gods that occasionally granted those requests.

The Gray Queen was none of those things. No one asked anything of the Queen, for she answered in thunder and in death. A few lucky souls might receive absolution and order, but for many, the Gray Queen's voice was the last thing their soul would ever hear. Bersk was no fool.

His only option—his last option—was to ask for permission to see Santa Anna.

Bersk stood and paced behind the tents and away from the crowd. Once he was alone, he groaned in frustration.

Pater O'Malley was right. He was a fool. There was no way that the bishops would let him see Santa Anna. He was a lowly sellsword—not even a Knight of Kripishi anymore—and she was a bishop about to be on trial. There was no way Bersk would get to see her before the other bishops were done interrogating her.

And yet, Bersk would ask to see her anyway. He had to.

"Protocol be damned," he muttered.

~ ~ ~

Chapter 9
Insects and Demons

AS NIGHT FELL, Kevril Bersk, Tamren Jorbough, Specialist Xandra, Sergeant Weylan, and a dozen other brave souls and experienced soldiers donned their armor and gathered their armaments.

Captain Besting gathered the hunter, bard, and the officers into his tent to discuss the plan. The five stood around the captain's table. All were restless.

"Are you sure that will be enough men?" Besting asked.

Bersk nodded. "Any more and we risk bogging ourselves down and diluting the magic. A small force is best."

"And Mr. Jorbough, you're quite certain that your magic can find the missing men?"

Tam nodded, arms crossed as if he were fighting the urge to stroke his beard.

Bersk added, "Xandra, Tam, and Archimedes will take a soldier or two and find the missing men—"

"Archimedes?" Xandra asked.

Tam replied, "His raven—not just a raven… It's complicated. Don't worry. You'll be happy we're taking it."

The hunter smirked and continued, "Tam will maintain the *tracking spell*, while Xandra holds *darkvision* on everyone.

"Weylan, you and the rest of the men will set blasting powder along both of our paths. Remember, we don't have to place charges in every tunnel. I'll take a portion with me to the main chamber to be sure the hive is good and buried. I'll maintain *hiding in plain sight*."

Weylan grumbled. "You're sure you're alright by yourself?"

Xandra interjected, "The hunter can take care of himself."

"I'm flattered," Bersk said, "but we're splitting our magic enough as it is."

Weylan said, "What if some of the Formicae survive? Can't they just dig back to the altar? What's to stop this happening all over again?"

Bersk replied, "Their queen was already on the altar, likely near death. There's no way she'll survive. The hive won't either. Some Formicae might survive, but they'll starve in a week or two."

The words fell harshly in the room, though Bersk didn't mean for them to. It was simply a sad fact at this point. He had tried not to think about it. An entire hive damned by the altar's demonic influence.

To their credit, each man and woman in the tent seemed to dwell on that knowledge.

"Very good then," Captain Henring said quietly. "Either way, we'll put a stop to this."

Bersk added, "Captain, you and the rest of the men should prepare to move camp. We don't know how far the hive stretches. The collapse could disturb the ground this far away. I suggest pulling the encampment back another quarter mile."

Henring nodded. "I suppose after this we'll be moving either way. Some of us back to Arkcaster to report. Some of us further across the plains to secure land. Very well, Mr. Bersk."

"What happens after?" Sergeant Weylan asked quickly, looking at the hunter.

All eyes fell on Weylan, and all but the Captain took the Sergeant's meaning. The Captain didn't know that Xandra and Weylan were vampyres, or that they were responsible for the nighttime deaths in camp.

Bersk cleared his throat. "Once we set the charges, we'll only have a few minutes to escape. If we encounter any snags, the priority is setting the charges; there's no point in saving the men down there just for us to fail and for more men to die later.

"We need to get this right. Whatever the altar wants with the Formicae queen… it's close. There won't be enough time to get more blasting powder from Arkcaster.

"After that, the hive collapses, the altar is buried, and we can all go our separate ways. Wherever the city needs you."

Though Bersk had met the eyes of each in the tent, he ended on the two officers so there would be no mistaking him. Bersk couldn't afford to have the two vampyres sandbagging and hiding their powers, or afford for them deciding to turn on him and the others in a crazed plan to hide the evidence of what they were.

The two officers nodded to him, and it seemed as if they might keep their sense about them. That was, unless being closer to the altar didn't persuade them otherwise.

~

When the moon was hanging in the sky and the sun all but set, Bersk, Tam, and the officers led the small force to the edge of the forest. Archimedes rode on the bard's shoulder, much to Tam's unease.

They watched the entrance to the Formicae hive for some minutes before continuing with their plan. It was roughly the same time of day when Bersk and Xandra had entered the hive behind a returning group of workers… but this night, the hive and the cliffs were completely still.

The group carried fifty pounds of blasting powder between them, divided amongst ten sacks. The powder was light, each canvas sack being roughly the size of a helmet and only five pounds each. Each man carried half a dozen fuses that could be lit at a distance with a simple fire spell and would give them roughly two minutes to vacate the area—a pitiful amount of time for a normal man, but with Bersk's *speed of the wind* spell they would survive.

Each cast their spells on the group: Xandra's and Tam's spells were first. The regular soldiers looked up and regarded the night sky with wonder—the stars were no doubt blazing brightly against the void. Meanwhile, Tam used a locket from one of the captured men to cast the *tracking spell.*

Only the officers looked at Bersk while he cast his first spell. His eyes dripped with blue from his goddess's *all-seeing order* spell. The night glowed bright blue, and several soldiers took a step back from him, including Sergeant Weylan. Bersk took a small amount of joy in causing the vampyre such distress.

While Tam bowed his head in concentration, Archimedes sat on Tam's shoulder and craned its head at Bersk. The hunter stared back at Archimedes and then looked through the psychopomp's eyes at himself.

Bersk couldn't remember the last time he had looked at himself in such a way or with the spell. With Archimedes so close, it looked as if he was staring at himself in the mirror. And the all-seeing order spell looked even more distressing than he remembered. The bright, electric blue color was unnatural, and his eyes were as solid and unreadable as glass.

Finally, Tam looked up at Bersk and breath caught in his throat. "I... I'd quite forgotten about that one," he said, staring at the blue holes in his friend's face.

Bersk turned to him, and in the light of the Gray Queen, he saw his friend with the same clarity as the vampyres—just a man. Not a soldier nor a vampyre. Not a Terran that should be delving into such a dangerous place. Though one of surprising resilience, and wiser and deeper beyond his years.

"Do you feel them?" The hunter asked, bringing them back to task.

Tam nodded, and Archimedes cooed on his shoulder. "Yes, I do."

"Very well," Bersk replied, looking at all of the group once more. "Remember the turns you take. We'll pause to set blasting powder, but otherwise follow Tam and I until our paths split... *Ambulare sine vestigio.*"

An eerie silence fell over the scene as magic muted the shuffling and whispers of the soldiers. Even Archimedes ruffled its feathers and opened its mouth in a caw, but no sound escaped.

Bersk motioned for them to follow, and the group descended into the maw of the hive.

~

The hunter led them down the tunnels, which glowed blue with his magical sight. The others followed close behind.

When the rear group was pausing to set blasting powder, each soldier would touch the shoulder of the one in front of them to communicate without words. They paused at each junction, thorough in their sabotage.

Halfway down, Bersk felt a hand on his shoulder and saw that Tam and Xandra's group was turning to leave. Bersk watched the bard disappear around the corner in the eerie magical silence. Thankfully, he would be able to watch their progress through the eyes of Archimedes, who was still perched on the bard's shoulder.

Bersk waved for Weylan's group to follow with the blasting powder and patted his arm to signal for double-time. They jogged from one junction to the next.

When they reached the final junction, Bersk signaled for Weylan's group to turn back. The officer stared stoically at him before nodding and waving for his men to follow.

Bersk watched through the eyes of the raven as Tam and Xandra's group came to the end of the tunnel and to a large sleeping room. Though the ceiling rose up only partially, the room stretched out to either side for fifty feet. The Formicae denizens littered the room, piled up against and on top of one another without a care. Most were motionless in slumber, but others twitched idly in primitive dreams.

In the room, there were winding paths between piles of Formicae. The largest were barely wide enough for two soldiers to walk abreast. So Tam led them single file, eyes half closed as he felt the guiding magic of his spell.

With any luck, their team would find the missing men soon. Either way, Bersk had no time to waste.

Bersk turned his sight back toward the tunnel in front of him and then he quickly descended the final passage, alone.

~

Once more, the hunter stepped silently into the main cavern, the enormous rib cage of a long dead serpent. Again, he felt the simmering of power long embedded in the stone.

Below, he could hear the muffled writhing of the Formicae queen against the confines of the profane altar.

Kevril Bersk stalked down the slope, quiet as a phantom.

Though the hunter was ready for battle, should the hive descend on him, the cavern was surprisingly still—the mutated scion nowhere to be seen.

Bersk had wondered if the Formicae would be on heightened alert after evening, but so much of the insect's complexity was derived from their queen. It wasn't surprising to Bersk that there weren't any patrols to greet them, nor that the mutated scion wasn't around either. By defiling their queen, the Formicae had inadvertently turned themselves simple.

Even if the lead scion had been granted intelligence or sovereignty, it couldn't hope to influence the hive, not like the queen could. In that, Bersk found hope that he and his soldiers would bring down the hive.

Bersk reached the base of the cavern and set to work placing charges of blasting powder. He rolled these into clumps and wedged them into crevices along the outer wall.

As the hunter did this, he half-watched through the eyes of Archimedes. Tam and Xandra's group had stepped carefully through the Formicae sleeping room. Sweat beaded on the bard's forehead. Tam pointed and in the distance four soldiers stood in a circle, their backs against one another—sleeping while standing up.

But Bersk was brought back to the cavern by the clacking steps of the giant scion—coming from the other side of the twisting stone and bone altar.

The hunter froze, listening carefully.

The scion was coming his way, walking around the altar toward the slope. Bersk wouldn't be able to make it up the slope and to the tunnel before the scion saw him.

So Bersk ran silently toward the altar, slipping around the other side of it to hide from the creature. Pressed close to the altar, the smell of sulfur became unbearable, but the hunter smelled something else… Through cracks in the bones of the altar came a sickly sweet smell—as if the trapped queen was rotting while she was alive.

More clacking steps came as the scion walked round the edge of the altar, and Bersk followed, keeping the massive structure between them. *Hidden in plain sight* masked his smell and sound, so as long as he stayed out of sight, he might've had a chance to sneak back out.

But as he snuck around the back of the altar, Bersk noticed scratches on the surface. At first, he assumed they were merely random, but the large etchings had a pattern to them—one of writing, but one the hunter didn't recognize.

Though Bersk wasn't a gifted linguist compared to most in the Church's order, he recognized a great many languages even if he couldn't read them. This one was foreign to him.

Bersk stared at the closest symbol to him and tried to commit the shape to memory. When he escaped the hive and reconvened with Pater O'Malley, he would ask the old priest about it.

Kevril Bersk shook his head. All things in due time.

Through the eyes of Archimedes, Bersk saw Tam's group leading the hypnotized soldiers out of the sleeping chamber. Each soldier had their hands on the shoulder of a captive, pushing and steering them along the paths to leave the chamber.

Another minute or two would get them to the main tunnel and onward to the surface.

So the hunter waited, his gaze split between the psychopomp and the altar.

A horrid scratching sound came from the other side of the altar—long and steady… The sound of the scion etching symbols into the stone and bone.

Bersk had heard and read plenty of firsthand accounts of demonic possession. It was similar to intrusive thoughts that accompanied various forms of madness and depression, except that there were also explicit feelings of paranoia as another being forced its way inside their mind. It was theorized to be similar to the way insect queens exerted their control over the denizens of the hive. Subtle urgings here, explicit commands elsewhere. The most disturbing part of these earlier stages was how subtle the process was—how often a victim would explain away changes in behavior or losses of control.

The most extreme possession was likened to being a passenger in their own mind. Of course, Terrans that were so deeply afflicted rarely survived.

Once a demon was so thoroughly embedded that it was taking control of its victim, the process only accelerated as the demon started altering their body and mind, warping their flesh with spells and wardings.

The final stages of metamorphosis were usually grotesque, like the scion that Bersk was currently hiding from.

As Bersk bided his time, half-watching Tam and Xandra's escape through the eyes of Archimedes and half-hiding from the scion, he wondered what the slow descent was like for the creature. Did the scion realize that there was another voice inside its head besides the Formicae ? Had it been conflicted when it turned against her? Had the demon convinced it that the queen was an intruder?

Was any part of the scion still in control or was it a passenger in its own mind? Did the scion struggle against the demon? Did it feel regret, sadness, or simply confusion now at what had become of itself and the queen?

Bersk shook his head. It didn't matter. None of it mattered.

Through Archimedes's eyes, Xandra's team passed the final junction. From there, they only had a few hundred feet to the surface. It was time to bring down the hive.

But before Archimedes could relay the signal, the hive rumbled—not with explosions, but with life.

Something must have happened with Weylan's group of soldiers.

Tam's group turned in shock. Specialist Xandra motioned for them to escape, then she turned and sprinted back into the depths of the hive.

Bersk grit his teeth in frustration, then willed Archimedes to follow. Without hesitation, the psychopomp flew through the tunnels, following just being the vampyre.

~

Bersk focused on himself, still in the main cavern and hiding behind the profane altar. On the other side, the possessed scion had stopped scraping runes into the stone and turned—

its dagger legs clacking against the cavern floor. It knew about the soldiers.

The time for subtlety was over. He reached out with magic and ignited the charges.

Bersk kept his goddess's *all-seeing order* spell, but silence wouldn't help the soldiers any longer. So Bersk dropped *hidden in plain sight*, and cast *step of the wind*. He wouldn't be able to cast it on anyone but himself, not while being so far away from the others. They would have to survive until Bersk could make it to them.

As Bersk cast the spell, the clacks of the scion's steps sounded again. The creature heard him, but now Bersk had the element of speed on his side.

The hunter conjured *Twitch*, rounded the mound of the altar and came face to face with the mutated scion. It reared back, towering above him, not bothering to flash its hypnotizing fins. It pointed two spear-tipped legs at him—its wounded leg already sprouting twin replacements.

It hissed and lunged for him. Bersk spun and slipped the first attack, dashing to its back legs in attempt to cripple the scion. But two tails swung down on him like bull-whips—the tail of the scion freshly split and oozing blood.

Bersk slashed with the blue blade, severing one tail and dodging the second. Then the hunter ducked below the scion's body, avoiding its legs whilst slashing at two of them. In the whirl of beast and hunter, Bersk managed to slash three of its hind legs.

The once towering scion slunk low to the ground, holding its two front legs up for defense and its single tail overhead like a scorpion. It chattered in pain or anger, but didn't lash out while Bersk stayed away from it.

He could've ended the scion, but each moment spent fighting was another that the men above might be overrun.

So Bersk turned and sprinted with magical speed up the cavern slope to the tunnels. The possessed scion screamed behind him.

~

The tunnels were a blur of blue as Bersk sprinted through with *Twitch* in hand.

In the fight with the scion, Bersk had lost track of Archimedes's location in the tunnels. All Bersk knew was that Archimedes had just caught up to Specialist Xandra, Weylan, and his squad.

Of the raven's many talents, at the moment Bersk needed only one. Its large and brutish Ugu form would be too large to fight in the narrow confines of the tunnel. So Bersk bid Archimedes to change into its Kisaga form.

Archimedes crowed into the tunnel, announcing itself before its voice became raspy and wet like the hiss of a snake. The raven fluttered to the ground, its body elongating, feathers turning to fur that shimmered with purple and shadow. Its face became the maw of a black jungle cat, but that was where its solid form ended. The body of the Kisaga was coiled shadow and void. One moment, it might slither across the walls like a weightless serpent and another moment, leap down and lash out with bladed tails conjured from its flanks. When speed was of the essence, the Kisaga was formless, fast, and violent.

As Archimedes finished shifting, Bersk lost his sighted connection to his guardian.

The hunter kept running.

Now workers and guard beetles were streaming out of the side tunnels and into the main passages. But Bersk didn't stop. He leapt over some with magical speed, spun around others, not bothering to slash at them with *Twitch*.

Bersk ran until he heard screams and violence. He nearly ran into the middle of the battle—a wall of guard beetles and workers were pushing against one another. Behind them, Bersk heard clashes of blades against armor.

The hunter willed Archimedes to him and, in a single breath, the formless black panther slithered over the mass of insects.

Together, Bersk and Archimedes became a whirlwind of violence. Bersk's steps and blade flashed with magic, slicing through Formicae chitin and moving to the next target before the first had a chance to drop. But the Kisaga was faster—even with magical sight, Bersk saw his guardian only in flashes of violence. It slithered between insects, rolling over them while conjuring bladed tendrils, reducing them to thrashing, limbless piles.

In moments, the hunter and the Kisaga had sliced their way through to the Xandra, Weylan, and the soldiers. The Terrans stood back to back, holding what ground they could. The few hypnotized Terrans stood in the center in vacant expressions.

Xandra and Weylan took most of the brunt. Both officers were a blur of steel. In the desperation of the moment, they'd given up hiding their abilities. Their supernatural powers were unshackled, their fangs pronounced.

As Bersk and the Kisaga reached them, the hunter recasted *speed of the wind* on all of them, and then yelled for them to run. Bersk and the Kisaga charged through the line of beetles, followed by Xandra and the soldiers. The regular soldiers grasped hold of the recently rescued and dragged them along while Weylan followed at the rear.

They swept like a rising flood through the hive and all those that stood in their way and burst out into the open night air.

~

Bersk had lost track of time, and so he shouted for the soldiers to run away from the hive and deep into the forest. Archimedes transformed back into its raven form, taking to the sky and overlooking the scene while they ran.

Not a minute later, the ground shook and then the clearing began to sink. Through Archimedes's eyes, Bersk saw the cliff-side rumble and give way. For a moment, the roar of the earth grew deafening, and Bersk feared that even with magic speed they hadn't run far enough—that the entire cliffside around the hive might collapse into a landslide.

Bersk held the *speed of the wind* spell, just in case, but the calamity passed. Deep in the forest, the ground sagged but the roots of the old trees helped hold the soil together. Much of the collapse was contained to the open plains.

~

As silence befell the group, Bersk looked at the soldiers. "You should take the others back to camp. The scion's hold over them should dissipate in a day or two, but until then, they should be monitored. We need to investigate the collapse."

All eyes fell to Specialist Xandra, the ranking officer. Though her fangs had receded, the soldiers still looked at her and Weylan with a mix of emotion. They had seen the vampyres—it didn't matter if the vampyres had fought on their side. The officers would no longer be able to hide amongst the military.

Bersk and Tam glanced between the officers and the enlisted soldiers, unease growing amongst them.

Finally, Xandra nodded, her shoulders sagging. "The sellsword is right. Take these men back to camp."

The soldiers reluctantly turned, all of them looking to Bersk, as if silently asking that he watch over them as they walked away. Meanwhile, Weylan watched the men go, and Bersk couldn't tell if he watched them as a senior officer or as a predator.

"That's it then," Weylan said, resentment in his voice. "The captain and the rest of the brigade will know now. All for four men…"

Bersk stared at the vampyre. Bersk still saw Weylan in a haze of blue, blood still staining the front of him. "Consider it the first half of your debt."

"What's the second?" the sergeant shot back. "Being burned at the stake?"

"Investigating the—"

Bersk was cut off by a rumbling in the distance. Through Archimedes's eyes, he saw stirrings in the crater of the hive. The dirt at the bottom began to sink.

"Come with me." Bersk ordered and ran down the slope.

For a moment, he considered that the vampyres might run. That they might escape into the forest before the rest of the brigade came for them. But to the officer's credit, Bersk heard the footsteps of them and Tam behind him.

They ran out of the treeline and stopped at the precipice of the crater. In the epicenter of the collapse—above the main cavern and the altar—the crater sank down fifty feet into the ground.

Deep at the bottom, the sinking of the ground seemed to grow wider and quicker—

Until a spear-point sprung from the depths. The group watched in quiet gasps as another sharp arm reached through, followed by the chattering face of the mutated scion. It stared at Bersk with a mix of inhuman and demonic anger.

"Look away!" Bersk shouted. *Twitch* was already in his hand and glowing fiercely in the moonlight.

Even with its demonic strength, the scion's climb was hard fought. Its neck and shoulders finally rose above the surface, and the colorful, hypnotizing fins that Bersk had worried about were broken and torn clean, revealing blue blood oozing from its sides.

But then the beast began to writhe. Rather than pulling itself further out, its sharp arms flailed and jabbed wildly at the ground. Its chattering mandibles opened wide in a drawn out shriek. Fear was written on the face of the scion.

Then despite its thrashing, it slid back beneath the surface as if it was being pulled under.

"That's not good," Tam said. "I thought the collapse would—"

"Stay behind me," Bersk said.

Just as the scion's head slipped beneath the ground and it seemed like the beast was gone forever, it burst forth out of the ground and into the air—

Clutched in the giant maw of the Formicae queen. Her long neck and torso rose into the air, swallowing the last bit of the possessed scion. The queen should've been a mix of both scion and guard beetle—a long lithe body covered with hard chitin armor. But as she slithered out of the ground, the full depths of her possession became clear.

Steam radiated from the pit and her body burned with corrupting influence. Her legs, the long slender legs of a spider, were instead coiling and whip-like, slithering across the ground like an octopus's limbs. The armor around her body was cracked and oozed bright blue blood, droplets of which dripped upward in the powerful heat. And instead of insect mandibles, her face was split open a dozen ways.

Kevril Bersk thought back to the frog demon brilgura from the tiny village of Keld—its pledge to the Mother of Demons, their second battle, and its misshapen body. Whatever altar had lain below the hive was immensely powerful for it to mutate the queen in such a way.

"What spells do you know, Xandra?" Bersk asked.

Beside him, her voice was barely a whisper. "Not much that will harm it."

To both Xandra and Tam, Bersk said, "Be frugal with your spells. Hex the queen if you can. Bolster us if you cannot."

"*Vires et voluntatem*," Bersk whispered, casting the spell of strength on himself and his allies. But even with the magical strength and confidence from the spell, the hunter felt apprehensive.

Tam muttered his hex spell—something to slow and confuse the queen's strikes. But then groaned in frustration. "Do what you can and do it quickly!"

Bersk said, "*Mora ordinem*," calling upon his goddess's spell of *Lingering Balance*. Then the hunter and the vampyres sprinted down the slope of the crater and fell upon the possessed Formicae queen in a fury. In the crater, the smell of sulfur was potent, enough that an unbolstered Terran would've choked on it.

Xandra and Weylan already had a vampyre's strength and speed. Coupled with Bersk's spell of strength, they were a force to be reckoned with. The mutated queen towered over them like a cobra, lashing out with her tendrils, swinging them in wide arcs or crashing them down on the slope with enough force to cause rockslides. The vampyres dodged them easily, swinging steel with hurricane force—cleaving completely through the ends of her tendrils.

But their swords couldn't penetrate the hard chitin of her body. Both Xandra and Weylan leapt dozens of feet into the air and onto her back in a single bound, but unless they struck the tender joints between plates, their swords were useless.

Meanwhile, Bersk ran around her belly, striking with the Gray Queen's sword—even as his skin screamed from the scalding demonic heat. Each slash left marks of *Lingering Balance* upon her. Each wound bled bright blue onto the ground and ate away at the queen's defenses.

And as the queen lashed out with tendrils to fend off Kevril Bersk, the vampyres defended him, cleaving through the arms of the queen.

The titanic insect writhed, undulating her body across the crater in attempt to crush the Terrans beneath her. Bersk narrowly avoided being crushed, all the while slashing at any part of her that came within his reach.

In minutes, the queen slowed under the combined might of the heroes, dripping blue from countless slashes across her. The chitin plates began to crumble and fall to the rocky ground, revealing tender gray flesh beneath. The bellows of the giant became high-pitched squeals. Even the blistering steam was subsiding.

The end was near.

As her armor fell away, Xandra and Weylan grew bold, aiming for the queen's exposed flesh. Now their steel cut her deep, spilling waves of blue blood from her flanks.

As the towering queen was brought low to the ground like a dying snake. Her cries grew weak.

And her body pulsed as if her insides were boiling.

Berk's eyes widened—whatever demon was possessing the queen wasn't done changing her.

"Get back!" Bersk shouted. "All of you!"

Tam was still at the top of the crater, and Bersk and Xandra ran back up the slope, putting distance between them and the changing queen. But Weylan kept attacking, relentlessly.

"Don't stop!" Weylan shouted. "She's nearly dead."

The Sergeant raised his blade and leapt, soaring through the air to the creature—

And a gray hand burst out of the queen and grasped Weylan by the throat—stopping him mid-flight. The vampyre writhed in its grip. The arm was thick with coiled muscle, shaped like a Terran's arm and covered with bony plates like that of the queen.

The arm retracted back into the creature, pulling the thrashing Weylan with it.

Xandra didn't even have time to scream before her counterpart was gone—disappeared inside the mass of flesh.

Bersk was frozen, Twitch in hand, unsure of what to do. He didn't have any magic that could pull the poor bastard out.

Meanwhile, the queen shuddered. Her mangled squid-like arms fell and her body writhed. Then her head fell low and the creature wretched. From her maw slithered mass of bile and bone. Midway down, Bersk saw Weylan, covered in muck, and still wriggling in the clutches of the thing. The smell of sulfur and heat rose again.

Then it stood. From the mass rose the approximation of a Terran. Its skin was gray, the body thick with pronounced bone and muscles that pulsed like snakes. The upper body was that of a four-armed Terran, one of which held Weylan fast, whilst the lower half of its body stretched on like the torso of a gray crocodile. A bundle of tails stretched out behind it, laying on the ground like a flail.

Specialist Xandra shouted, *"fulgur lancea!"* Lightning crackled from her fingertips and blasted across the crater. Each shot reverberated through the air, leaving streaks of smoke in the sulfur-heavy air. The bolts pierced the torso of the demon, and sailed into the rock behind it. The demon shook but stood unperturbed.

Bersk's eyes fell upon the demon's face—no more than a skull with skin. Lidless eyes stared back.

The demon said, "Hello Kevril Bersk. Mother Ariazi sends her regards." Its voice was wild and horrid, like a horse being burned alive.

Weylan's flailing grew weak and feeble.

"Fast and decisive!" Bersk shouted, followed by, *"Astar na gaoithe."* In the same moment, he willed Archimedes to change back into a Kisaga.

Somewhere behind them at the top of the crater, Tam cast a spell too, a luck spell.

Kevril Bersk and Specialist Xandra sprinted across the crater in a blink, both enhanced by magical speed, the sleek formless body of the Kisaga beside them.

Xandra conjured electricity as she ran, bolt after bolt snapping and leaving fiery streaks in the air. Each falling weakly against the demon's hide.

Archimedes got to the demon first and swirled across its body like churning black water punctuated by the slashes of blades. The demon recoiled in shock of the assault. It swiped wildly with its other three arms, as if it were covered with stinging insects.

Bersk leapt through the air, aiming for its fourth arm that was still holding Sergeant Weylan by the throat. *Twitch* flashed brilliantly across the demon's wrist—its hand and the sergeant both falling lifelessly to the ground.

The demon shrieked loud and high, like the boiling scream of a kettle condensed into a single moment. It turned and lunged for Bersk with all three good arms, and when the hunter slipped its grasp, it lunged again with snapping teeth.

Xandra's magic assault was forgotten as the vampyre slipped close to the crazed demon, using the distraction to pull the lifeless Weylan away from the battle.

Red blood oozed freely from the demon now, as the Kisaga continued scurrying across its body and rending it, but in spite of the damage, its focus was entirely on Bersk. It swung wilding, its fingers elongating into claws. The hunter slipped and dodged its strikes, backpedaling and ducking under its stampeding torso. Each time, lashing out with *Twitch*. Soon, the bleeding torso of the demon was covered in dripping blue.

In spite of his superior speed, thrice Bersk felt the helping nudge of Tam's luck magic saving him from direct blows.

Moments later, Xandra continued her magical assault. Now, each bolt caused the demon to stutter as it chased Bersk around the crater. Chunks of gray bone and flesh splattered across the rocks.

And the demon diminished. With each passing moment, the demon grew smaller and smaller from its injuries. The towering creature was soon no taller than the hunter that it pursued.

The demon leaned back and screeched again, bright red blood frothing from its mouth. Then it turned and shouted, *"Oriri ossaterrae!"*

The crater trembled and rocky pillars burst from the ground, rising twenty feet into the air. Each was as thick around as a man, as numerous as wheat, and rose at odd angles, crashing into others and forming a tangled mass of stone. Bersk twisted his body to avoid being smashed between two columns, then leapt high into the air to perch atop another.

The Kisaga crawled upward to Bersk and shifted back into Archimedes, its magic nearly spent. It perched on the hunter's shoulder.

Bersk breathed deep and scratched the raven's head. "Good job, *somnamica*."

Meanwhile, the demon slithered through the tangled stone of the crater.

"We can't let him escape," Bersk whispered and willed the bird to follow from the sky. Archimedes flew off.

The screeching voice of the demon sounded again as it left the twisted columns and raced up the slope. *"Restu sonmova, liberomeo."*

Bersk turned to the vampyres and found them both standing side by side, heads bowed. Completely motionless.

The hunter raced to them. He didn't recognize most of the words of the spell and so he didn't know what exactly it had done. He only recognized one word:

Children.

Bersk leapt along the tops of the columns, then raced up the slope to the rest of his comrades. Tam stepped out from behind a tree.

"Did you see where it went?" Tam asked.

Bersk nodded and said, "Archimedes is following it." Then he set to shaking the shoulders of the vampyres. But they did nothing—merely stared at the down at the ground.

"Stay with them," the hunter said, turning to run.

Tam grabbed Bersk's sleeve. "Is that wise?"

"No, but I can't let it escape."

~

Bersk sprinted through the forest, moving fast as a predator with his magically enhanced speed.

High above, Archimedes followed the demon. Through the dense trees, it saw only glimpses, but that was enough.

As the hunter found the path of the demon, broken saplings and shed skin—lots of shed gray skin.

Minutes later, Bersk came upon a lanky, naked Terran, sprinting through the brush. Bersk ran around wide and then stopped in front of the man.

His body was completely hairless, his skin pale and slick with sweat or slime. His face was deep set, nearly gaunt. But where his face showed the faint wrinkles of age, the skin of his body was eerily smooth.

The demon stared back at Bersk with a growing smile that showed eerily human teeth. In spite of its power, the demon stood with an absence about it—not regally or relaxed, nor nervous. Like a commoner waiting about the market.

Bersk held *Twitch* between them. Though this new form *looked* less imposing than the last, looks meant little when it came to demons.

"Impressive," Bersk said. "I've never seen one of your kind change so quickly." When the man moved to walk around Bersk, the hunter leveled the blade at the creature. "I'm not sure where you think you're going, demon, but your journey ends here."

The demon turned and began to pace slowly. "I was thinking of going South. Maybe stop at the little hamlet on my way to Arkcaster."

All traces of demonic influence were gone from its voice, and as it paced, it showed its back idly to the hunter.

"What are you?" Bersk asked, trying not to let the apprehension show in his voice. "You're no low rung soldier. What's your name?"

"Why Kevril, I'm flattered. Most humans were too naive to show such an interest in me. Most hunters were much too quick."

"Your name, creature."

"First, tell me the year."

Bersk shifted on his feet. "1722 in the year of Our Lord. 3892 by the High Mages. 5313 in the Elven calendar."

The demon's eyes narrowed. "In *my* calendar."

Bersk's sword arm felt heavy. Only two types of demon told time by the demonic calendar: The very dumb and the very old.

"Your name," Bersk said again.

A wide smile crept across the demon's face. "No. Why don't you run on back to the Church, Kevril Bersk. Pater O'Malley knows my name, and Santa Anna is waiting for you."

The hunter's unease gave way to anger. "You'll regret that. *Vetiti ordinis: Ororrim effigies.*"

Bersk became many. Ten copies of himself appeared from the ether and surrounded the demon. Ten copies of *Twitch* glowed brightly in the night.

"The Gray Queen will not suffer your existence on this plane. Any last words?" The words echoed from all ten copies simultaneously.

But the demon just smiled. "Did you see what I did to the vampyres back there? All of my children answer to me, whether they want to or not… How long do you think it would take for them to tear Tamren Jorbough apart?"

Bersk's skin felt cold and his breath caught in his throat. "You're bluffing," six of the copies said.

"Am I?"

Bersk stared at the creature. He knew that the thing in front of him was no ordinary demon—that even now, even with the power of his goddess, Bersk had a sliver of a chance of defeating it.

There was no chance he could defeat the demon before it took the life of his friend.

Would it kill Bersk instead? Was this a trade? Bersk's mortality slowly descended upon him, like a dark curtain being drawn.

"Is this a trade?" four of the copies asked. "My life for the bard's?"

Above them, Archimedes cawed in dissatisfaction.

The demon walked toward him—one of him.

Bersk's heart pounded in his chest and even with the forbidden magic of the Gray Queen, the hunter felt fear.

"Get out of my way, Kevril Bersk."

The copy stepped aside and the demon walked past.

"Smart human."

The magic of the forbidden Mirror Image spell was already fading, and with it, the time to strike.

The hunter sighed and let the magic fade. The copies of himself disappeared into the ether.

Bersk turned, dumbfounded, and watched the demon walk off into the woods. When it was gone, he turned and ran back to the crater—back to his friend.

~ ~ ~

Chapter 10
Mortals and the Rest

KEVRIL BERSK EMERGED from the treeline into the moonlight and found the vampyres and Tam waiting for him at the edge of the crater. Whatever holding magic had been used on Specialist Xandra and Sergeant Weylan was long gone with the demon.

Weylan was holding Tam from behind, one arm across the bard's chest, pinning his arms down, and the other hand around his throat.

Xandra was facing them. "Let him go, Weylan. That isn't the way."

But Weylan was already looking at the hunter. Moments later, all eyes fell to Bersk as he approached.

Weylan bared his teeth. Sweat beaded on the vampyre's forehead and he stepped back uneasily, dragging Tam with him. The bard winced and held fast to Weylan's wrist, the heels of his shoes sliding across the ground.

Xandra turned to Bersk and raised her sword. "Stop there, hunter." Though her voice was firm, tears welled in her eyes.

Bersk stopped and willed *Twitch* away. He stood, arms outstretched. "You can let the bard go, Weylan. I'm unarmed."

Weylan glanced up to the sky, looking for Archimedes. "Somehow I doubt that, Mr. Bersk. Where's your bird?"

"The raven is following the demon. And I'm as unarmed as I can be." When neither Xandra nor Weylan moved, Bersk added, "What are you doing? What do you think is going to happen here?"

Xandra glanced back, but it was Weylan who spoke.

"We're leaving with your friend."

"I've got a better idea," Bersk said, frustration bleeding into his voice. "Let the bard go, and you both run before the rest of the soldiers get here."

Weylan shook his head. "The captain—the whole brigade—knows what we are now! Do you really think they'll let us go after what we did?"

"I don't care," Bersk said sternly. "But you've paid your debt to me. Don't sully it now."

"How can we trust you? How do we know that you won't hunt us down with your bird?"

"Don't go back to Arkcaster," Bersk said. "The demon said that it is going there."

"What?" Weylan asked, eyes widening in disbelief.

"I don't care where you go… Just leave my friend alone."

Xandra whispered harshly, "Weylan, I can hear them. We need to go. *Now.*"

Meanwhile, Bersk and Weylan locked eyes. It took another breath, but the sergeant finally released Tam. The bard stumbled, gasping for air.

The vampyres disappeared across the plains and into the forest. True to his word, Bersk didn't follow them, nor will Archimedes to follow them.

Bersk ran to Tam. "Are you alright?"

Tam nodded quickly and cleared his throat several times. "I tried to tell him to hold me hostage some other way. If my voice is off, I'll have to find him and press him for damages."

Both men shared an uneasy laugh.

The hunter turned his gaze to Archimedes. The raven was nearly a mile away now, searching for the demon. By some power or magic, it had slipped from Archimedes's sight, much to the raven's dismay.

"Damn."

"What's that?" Tam asked, standing up and brushing himself off.

"The demon's gone."

"You're losing your touch." When Bersk didn't smile at the joke, Tam patted his shoulder and added, "No matter. I'm sure you'll find it soon enough… Bersk?"

The hunter met Tam's eyes. "This wasn't an ordinary demon. Not like a little one or a… lonolan, or like the brilgura."

Shouts and footsteps echoed through the trees—the sound of the brigade. They approached, blades drawn.

"Fan out! Search the treeline!" Captain Henring barked, pushing his way to the front. "Bersk! What happened? What about the demon and the vampyres?" He walked toward the crater and peered over.

The hunter said, "They got away."

Henring turned, eyes narrowed. "Which ones?"

"All three," Bersk replied, dejection seeping into his voice. "The demon fled South. Said something about heading to Arkcaster…" He pointed off to the treeline. "Your two soldiers went that way, but they're long gone by now."

"But you can track them, can't you? We'll hunt them down the old-fashioned way."

Bersk shook his head. "Sir, you need to get word to Arkcaster as quickly as possible."

"Don't presume upon me, hunter. I want you to follow—"

"*Captain*, this is no ordinary demon. It's finished its transformation. It looks like a man now, just like you or me. Except that it's not a man or a vampyre, or a lycan, or anything so charming. When it reaches your city, its power will only grow. It will corrupt Terrans and monster alike. It will fester in Arkcaster like a rotting wound.

"Would you damn your entire city for vengeance?"

Bersk's voice had risen loud enough for all the nearby soldiers to hear—a dozen of which stood behind the Captain, staring intently at their commanding officer.

Captain Henring's glare softened, slowly undermined by muted horror and uncertainty.

"On my word as a hunter, you cannot wait."

Henring stared off across the forest and nodded reluctantly. "Very well, Bersk. We'll do this your way. We'll double-time back to Arkcaster."

"I'll get word to the Church. They'll send word to the branch in Arkcaster."

Henring smirked half-heartedly. "With any luck, the Council and the Church will work together."

Bersk turned to Tam, who stood with hands clasped, like a soldier awaiting orders.

"What about me, Bersk?" the bard asked, stoically, as if his life hadn't just been threatened.

"If you're up for it, I need you with me in Arkcaster."

Tam nodded. "Say no more. Captain Henring, might I accompany your brigade a little further?"

Henring nodded, turned, and began calling back his men.

Meanwhile, Bersk was left with his friend.

"I'm sure the lad Stanberry will be glad to hear that."

Tam winced and stifled a laugh. "And I'm sure the rest of them won't."

And as the moment wore on, Bersk found himself dwelling on the sight of his friend in the clutches of a vampyre. That such a moment might happen again.

Bersk said quietly, "Let me know when I ask too much. Do me that favor."

Tam smiled reluctantly. "I will."

~

While the soldiers and Tam prepared to leave and before Bersk teleported to the Septriones Church, the hunter trudged back down the slope to the bottom of the crater.

Bersk had thought that burying the altar would be enough, but after witnessing the demon's power first hand, he thought better of it. Burying it would just leave the problem for a later generation. A lesser gateway might have been forgivable…

The hunter knelt on the rocks at the bottom of the crater and conjured *Twitch*. The itching discomfort left his hand while Bersk drew the sigils of order in the dirt. Minutes later, he'd finished the interlocking sigils.

Bersk held out Twitch and spoke the old words.

"By the will of the Gray Queen, I am her hand and her voice.

I stand upon the shoulders of The Dead Prince,
Spurned by the Realm That Has No Name.
We impose the Balance upon this cursed land."

And in the final line, two other voices overlapped his—the voice of the Prince and the voice of the Queen.

Molten blue dripped steadily from the sword and coalesced into the lines of the sigil. The glow retreated from the sword, leaving dull steel in its wake.

And when all the ether had shifted from the sword to the runes, Bersk finished the incantations.

"By the will of the Gray Queen, erase this madness." the three voices said.

The crater shuddered and groaned, the tremors becoming violent as the power of the Gray Queen reached deep into the ground. From the rocks rose the ancient altar of stone and bone. And as it rose above Bersk, the precipice of it was shorn off. The altar crumbled as fast as it rose and soon fractured pieces of it were piling up around the crater. The blue power of the Gray Queen seeped out of the broken edges and puddled in the crater—the pieces melting and becoming unrecognizable.

And as the base of the altar rose up and subsequently crumbled, both the rumbling and the blue faded.

The glowing blue in the sigils leapt from the ground back to Twitch, coating it in the eerie glow.

"Order come, and Gray Queen's will be done."

Somewhere in the distance, Archimedes crowed with satisfaction.

~

When the ground had settled and the Arkcaster brigade was marching away, Bersk called Pater O'Malley with his lodestone.

Moments later, the hunter appeared in the Septriones Church, surrounded by rocky walls and everlit candles.

O'Malley looked up from his Enchiridion. His face wrinkled in concern. "What happened? Is it the altar?"

"The altar is gone, but a demon came through."

"And…?"

Bersk grit his teeth. "It escaped. It's heading for Arkcaster. It's… I think it's a Demon Lord."

Pater O'Malley stood and grabbed the Demonicon from his bookshelf. The thick tome was bound in leather, with old words gouged in red across it. "Tell me everything."

Bersk recounted the runes upon the altar, fight with the demon and the subsequent chase through the woods—how it changed forms so quickly. That it asked for the demonic calendar, and how easily it influenced two vampyres. Then Bersk said, "The demon said you would know its name."

O'Malley had been flipping through the thick tome, and paused. He shook his head in confusion, then he stared at Bersk, his eyes widening.

"What is it?" the hunter asked.

"There are hundreds of demons that have been cataloged and subsequently banished since the founding of the church. Hundreds, Bersk. Two dozen lords. I've only banished one: Josephite. But what you've described is far beyond what Josephite was capable of."

O'Malley flipped through the pages in great chunks now, flipping to the back of the book. He muttered, "It could be one of the Desolate Family. Maybe the Son or the Bastard—"

Bersk suddenly felt very cold. His mouth was dry as he sti-fled a chuckle. "Come now. You're joking."

O'Malley stopped and scanned the page with his finger, hand shaking as he did. "No. No," he muttered. "Oh, holy fa-ther. It's him. *Belial*—the son of Ariazi."

Before Bersk could offer counter or even muffled disbelief, O'Malley read from the book:

"Lo' and tremble before the Son of all demons. He shall be born of his mother's bones, brought forth by the unknowing and the unwilling. And he shall know of the form of demon and man. With purest thought, he commands the lowly among the demon-blooded as a general of the damned. He will walk among the Terrans, planting seeds of otherworldly evil that will hatch like parasitic chicks…

"He seeks a conduit between worlds. He is the herald of the Desolate. The first born of Ariazi shall bring forth the Mother of all demons."

O'Malley's voice had risen to a crescendo and then fallen like an executioner's axe, cleaving silence between the two men. Moments passed, and the two stared uneasily at one an-other.

The hunter's sword hand itched with discomfort beneath the glove.

"First thing's first," Bersk said. "I need salve. And then words."

~

Bersk knelt in front of the desk, removed his glove, and placed his right arm down before the priest.

O'Malley put on his own thin gloves and muttered the old words of healing over the bottle. Then he poured the salve over Bersk's gnarled forearm and worked it into his skin, starting from the elbow and moving downward.

"Why now?" Bersk asked. "I thought the Coming of Ariazi was hundreds of years from now?"

O'Malley worked as he spoke. "That's the common notion—the one they tell the new converts. But there *isn't* a date given, not even in the demonic calendar."

"Why the misdirection?"

The priest shrugged. "Why deal with today what can be put off until tomorrow?" He paused to mutter more arcane words.

Bersk snorted and waited. Then he said, "The truth for me but not for thee."

O'Malley looked up, and his massage slowed around Bersk's wrist. "Prophecies are an inexact science—you know that. Better the people think that the Lord is infallible. Doubt is poisonous."

"The Church must preserve its illusion."

O'Malley shook his head. "I'm not getting into another debate, Bersk." The priest had started on his palm and added, "Besides, the people do not want to know such terrible things, so let them think such things are far away."

"But they aren't given the choice—" Bersk groaned in frustration and left his thought. "It doesn't matter. What's our course of action now?"

"We need to speak with the bishops. If this really is the Coming of Ariazi, then the Church will need to bring all its forces to bear."

"On that, we agree."

O'Malley finished with the salve, and Bersk put his glove back on.

"So, what are we waiting for, then?" Bersk asked.

Pater O'Malley regarded him wearily and placed the bottle of salve back in his desk.

"I think I should speak with the bishops," the priest replied. "Alone."

"Nonsense. We don't have time for this—"

"Bersk, they won't speak to you."

"Then *they* can turn me away."

O'Malley stared at him. "Is that really why you want to see them?"

Bersk stared back. He thought of the demon's words. He asked, "Is she here?"

The priest scoffed. "I knew it."

"When did she get back, and why didn't you send for me?"

"Well, I thought until a moment ago you were fighting a demon! And... Archleon Greghan forbade you to see her."

Bersk's leather glove squeaked as his hands clenched in frustration. Bersk had to remind himself to breathe. "I'll ask him myself."

"Bersk, you forget your place—"

"No. You forget yours, Pater. It's my will. *My will.* The old bastard can rebuke me, himself."

Both men stood, chairs scraping against the stone floor. The air seemed to boil between them.

"We have other concerns—Bersk, don't you dare turn away from me. The world could be at stake! Collect yourself." O'Malley slammed the Demonicon shut and stormed around the desk. "Fine. Ask him—but not until we report this first. And if the archleon doesn't wish to speak to you on either account—"

Bersk held up his gloved hand. "*Enough.* I'm not your student anymore. Lead the way, *Pater.*"

A moment later, Pater O'Malley stormed past and led them through the underground halls of the Septriones Church. The Pater muttered half-hearted greetings to other clergy who poked their heads out of doorways to investigate the argument. Bersk didn't look at any of them.

It wasn't until they'd walked several twists and turns of passages that Bersk's teeth and fist finally unclenched.

~

Bersk wasn't sure how far the tunnels sprawled beneath Septriones Church, only that he was surprised by the length of the journey every time he went to the surface levels. Pater O'Malley's study was three levels down, and the priest had hinted that there were many more below that. Bersk assumed there were others too—truly secret rooms that were completely walled off and only accessible by lodestone—but he had never been allowed to see them. Now he likely never would.

A dozen turns later, they emerged above ground in the back enclaves of the Septriones Church. For a moment, Bersk was taken aback by the sight of it. The room, the whole of Septriones and any other church for that matter, were built in marble and crusted in gold. Dappled light shone through the stained glass windows and across the array of desks carved from exotic woods. Every surface depicted history, from the deep layered carvings of holy wars across the railings and pillars of long deceased heads of the church, to the rainbows of glass depicting events of creation that never were.

Bersk shook his head. It was beautiful, pompous, and built on lies.

Pater O'Malley and Bersk walked past the other priests and two archleon, clad in their golden robes. Several worked, others talked. All of which paused at the sight of the two men—

At the sight of a hunter that no longer worked for the Church, that no longer believed.

Whispers sounded as the pair walked through the ornate doors and into the connecting halls. Inside, the light reflected a dozen times off of the shining gold walls, and grew so bright it was nearly blinding; it was supposed to simulate communing with the Lord. And supposedly, the priests, who were closer to Him did not have to squint as much as they passed through.

But this time, Bersk glanced at Pater O'Malley and saw that his seigneur was also shielding his eyes.

Mercifully, their journey through the hall was short, and they entered the main wing. The hall sprawled outwards and upwards. Three massive glass chandeliers hung from the ceiling and burned with magic flame as if they were funeral pyres. Here were dozens more church heads, squires and initiated Knights of Kripishi, and other sprinkles of dignitaries.

Bersk shuddered, for in spite of the obvious differences the scene called forth images of the Formicae hive.

Off the sides of the hall lay the wing of archleons—filled with their private studies—and another for the columen. The latter of which were glorified guest rooms, since the columen were among the highest ranks and each had permanent residence in their native church.

Again, the pair walked with purpose, directly to the wing of the archleons. They found Archleon Greghan's study midway through the horseshoe-shaped passage.

Bersk considered standing outside the door, but Pater O'Malley knocked and said, "Leo Greghan, we have something urgent for you."

"Yes, and who is this *we*, O'Malley?" came the impatient voice from beyond.

The priest turned to Bersk and motioned for him to step inside the study. The hunter reluctantly followed.

While the lowly priests were confined to the hollowed out caverns below, the archleons got their own gold encrusted studies. Greghan's, and many others, were furnished ornately: The furniture was made of rich woods, the floors covered in lush carpets and furs, while the shelves were lined with artifacts and trinkets—all of it pilfered from various corners of the world.

And at the center of it all, sat Archleon Greghan. Bersk felt him the personification of the Church's opulence. His robe was gold and trimmed in jewels. The man himself was soft and scarless befitting a life of decadence that most rulers would never know. He peered back at Bersk, a scowl growing across his lips at the sight of the *former* Knight of Kripishi.

"Archleon," Bersk said flatly, doing his best to suppress his own disdain.

Greghan turned back to the priest. "This had better be good, O'Malley."

In a measured voice, the priest recounted Bersk's encounter with the altar and the demon, as well as their theory that the demon was Belial, the son of Ariazi.

Greghan's face twitched several times through the tale, and he glanced at Bersk twice before turning back to the priest.

The priest omitted much of the vampyres' involvement but summarized well. When he finished, he moved to set the De monicon down on the desk, but Greghan held up a hand to stay him.

"I know the prophecies," the fat archleon said, as he leaned back in his chair. "It's heading for Arkcaster?"

"Yes," O'Malley replied, speaking for the both of them.

Greghan rapped his fingers hard on the wood. "I understand your concern, O'Malley, and thank you for bringing this to me. I'll need to consort with the other diocese." Greghan rose from his chair. "Come with me. I trust you can recount this information again."

"Of course, but Kevril Bersk was the one—"

"I trust you can recount this information again."

"Yes, Leo."

"Good." Then Greghan glanced at Bersk and waved a dismissive hand. "That will be all."

"Leo," the hunter began, "I seek an audience with Santa Anna."

Greghan turned to O'Malley. "Didn't you tell him?"

"I did."

"He did," Bersk added.

"Then I don't see what else needs saying," Greghan walked around the table, between the two men, and out into the hall.

"Leo Greghan—"

"That will be all, *former* Knight of Kripishi."

Greghan cast an apathetic look at Bersk, and the rage boiled in the hunter.

There could not have been a greater disparity between the two men or of their opinions of one another. Bersk disliked the entirety of the archleon and had since his early training—everything Greghan was and everything he stood for. Bersk knew that Greghan's own disdain did not run as deep. To Greghan, Bersk was merely a broken tool—something looked down on in annoyance.

Greghan walked off, and Pater O'Malley glanced back toward Bersk, but couldn't bring himself to look his former student in the eye. Then O'Malley walked off, leaving Bersk alone in the golden hall.

~

Kevril Bersk walked through the golden hall and then through the Septriones main hall. Then he pushed through the giant double doors that led to the gardens.

Sunlight hit him forcefully and the hunter breathed deep. It was spring on Eadruin—this side of the world. The air was warm and thick, yet still pleasant.

After his eyes adjusted, he looked upon the sprawling gardens. They were a mix of gray stone and green hedges. In the distance, sepulchers peeked over hedges, rising like islands on top of the green sea. Occasional grave markers towered like spikes. In the distance, buildings from the side wings of the grounds could just be seen.

Bersk had forgotten how sterile the outside looked. There was color to be found, of course, but the succulent flowering plants were tucked away in meditation spots and private gardens—more treasures reserved for the servants of the Lord.

Above, the sky was an ominous tinge of green.

The hunter sighed and walked down the stone steps past idle priests, knights, and honor guards. Most paid him no mind. He strode into the gardens.

It had been a long time since he'd felt so powerless. For a moment, he considered that the last time might have been when he last spoke with Santa Anna, but that wasn't right. He smirked, for the last time was likely on these grounds, once again idly pacing the gardens while someone else decided his fate. Probably when he renounced the Order of Kripishi.

There was irony in there somewhere, Bersk was sure of it.

He sought solitude and walked along the wide stone path, brushing his hand along the hedges.

~

Some years ago, he'd walked these same stones with Santa Anna. Years… Had it really been so long?

Bersk drifted back as he walked, back to those walks that he'd replayed many times in his head. Familiar, yet always drifting further and further away.

The last time they walked these stones, Anna had talked about leaving—about crossing the Gelid Sea to the Frozen Isles. Starting the chain of events that would lead to her indictment and extradition. What she hadn't known was that Kev had planned on leaving, too.

Bersk had done his best to listen that day while Anna told him about her upcoming journey, but Kev's mind was clouded by earlier events. Plagued by his first encounter with the Gray Queen.

Kevril Bersk had already had doubts about his service to the Church and about his belief, but that chance encounter with the Mistress of Order had crystallized it—given it an overwhelming and unshakeable form.

The hunter felt a pang of regret that he did not remember the words of his Anna clearer.

If Bersk had known that would be the last time he would see Anna for years, would he have tried harder to listen, to commit her words to memory.

Bersk knew. He knew that nothing would've helped. For the Gray Queen had cast such a shadow over his life that the goddess had blotted out most everything else.

Yet, there was a difference between what he felt in the shadow of the Gray Queen and what he felt in the shadow of the Church. The Church was nothing more than Terrans and magic, acting with a unified will. If there was a Lord as they so claimed, Bersk had never felt its touch, had never heard its whispers or felt its guidance.

But by the forgotten gods, he had felt the presence of the Gray Queen! Seeing her had been like waking from a dream, like lightning coursing through his chest, like a child witnessing death for the first time or a mother giving birth. Kevril Bersk had struggled to remember the details of that beautiful and horrific encounter—all he could remember were the feelings that swirled within him. And that he had not been the same since.

It seemed impossible that such a thing could overshadowed the woman he loved, but it had. By the forgotten gods, it had.

Now the return of the demons had done it all over again.

~ ~ ~

Epilogue
The Grace of Prophets

KEVRIL BERSK WALKED to the edge of the stone path. The left side of the hedges gave way to a small overlook. Below, the Septriones gardens sprawled into the distance. Beyond that, the rolling hills continued to the horizon. In the distance, Bersk thought he could just make out the spires of the next citystate.

"I see someone else has a taste for solitude."

Bersk turned to see a columen approaching from farther down the path. He was alone, and exceedingly young for the station, even more so than Santa Anna. His face tan and his smile bright. His robes were a bright mix of bronze and orange.

"It's easier than the alternative," the hunter replied, wondering if he should bow.

"Ah, but are we ever truly alone?" The man approached, expressionate brow raised in question.

"It depends on the Terran's faith," Bersk replied, eyeing the columen both curiously and suspiciously. He stopped and stood next to the stone railing.

Bersk guessed that it must be Columen Devery. Bersk hadn't kept abreast of many changes within the Church, but he did know of the young man's meteoric rise to pillarhood—the youngest to ascend since Santa Anna.

"And do the gods speak to you, Kevril Bersk?"

Bersk suppressed his surprise. "More often than columen do. ...How did you know?"

Devery smirked—something playful and disarming. "You're the only warrior without a sword."

The hunter nodded and the statement hung pregnant in the air. Both men stood off center—both half-facing the view and each other.

Devery asked, "So, what brings you out to the gardens? Not many walk these paths alone."

Bersk hesitated, not wanting to lie, nor overstep. "I ran into a demon, and thought it necessary to bring the concern to Pater O'Malley."

Devery nodded, considering this. He stared out over sprawling hills, and Bersk thought for a moment that the columen had forgotten all about him.

"It's interesting," Devery began. "The things we choose to say and the things that we don't. Things omitted speak volumes more than words ever could." He turned to Bersk. "It must be concerning... I trust that Leo Greghan is bringing it before the other Dioceses?"

Again, Bersk suppressed his surprise. "Yes. Forgive me, Excellency—"

"Think nothing of it. The dioceses will debate amongst themselves, but eventually they'll bring it before the columen.

I'll feign ignorance." Devery flashed a smile, and Bersk couldn't help but return it.

"You've done well for yourself," Bersk said, relaxing. "I'm starting to see why."

At that, Devery's smile gave way to modesty. "Part of my role is vassal. The other part is knowing people." The columen looked at him out of the corner of his eye. "I trust you know that Santa Anna has been apprehended, and that she's returned?"

At the mention of Anna, Bersk felt his straight face slip. He frowned, more at himself than at anything else.

"I'm aware."

"You two were close."

Bersk hesitated. "We spoke between missions..."

Columen Devery saw through it. He smiled that disarming smile—one more befitting a barkeep than a man of the cloth.

"I know that you spoke often to each other. Nearly as often as you spoke to your seigneur and more often than you spoke to your Archleon Greghan. Though, I do not blame you.

"Further, I know that your conversations were innocent enough, but then the things we don't say matter so much more, don't they?"

Bersk's face felt flush and the hunter turned toward the rolling hills. "In the end, I'm not sure they matter at all, Excellency."

"Don't worry," Devery said, stepping closer. "If every servant of the Lord was kicked out for such a minor infraction, well... Is that why you left that Order?"

The hunter smirked. "You know that's not the reason."

Devery shrugged. "As I said."

Bersk was suddenly aware of how close Devery was standing—conspiratorially close. Bersk stepped back from him.

"Columen Devery, it's been an honor to meet you—"

"I'm going to see Santa Anna," he said abruptly. "I thought you might like to accompany me."

Bersk stood there, mouth agape, and when Devery didn't smile, Bersk scoffed instead.

"What are you playing at?" Bersk asked as steadily as he could manage.

"You come to Septriones, bringing news of the Desolate Family—all this despite your excommunication and Archleon Greghan's disdain for you. You are an eyewitness and a formidable spellblade. You will no doubt be called forth to accompany Knights of Kripishi to track the creature down.

"Furthermore, you are a confidant of the recently apprehended Santa Anna—who returns home *on the same day* as the demon's emergence. It behooves me to better know the man who is either at the center of coincidence or at the center of something else."

Bersk stared at the columen, words hanging between them in the garden. Finally, he said, "Archleon Greghan has forbidden it."

Devery smiled. "I am both his superior and in charge of Santa Anna's investigation. Walk with me."

Kevril Bersk walked beside the columen back up the stone path. All the while, he thought about what Devery had said, and all the things that he might've omitted.

END

NEXT TIME ON
*The Sword of the
Gray Queen*
Book 3:

Scourge of the Son
Available February 2023

Spoiler–Free excerpt from

Scourge of the Son

Footsteps sounded behind him, and Bersk whirled around, far more startled and more eager than he should've been.

Pater O'Malley stood at the sepulcher entrance, looking as surprised as Bersk was. O'Malley asked, "Were you expecting someone else?"

"No," Bersk replied, unconvincingly.

O'Malley face softened and he looked up at the sky. Bersk wondered if he was debating whether to comment on his protege or if he really missed seeing the clouds that much.

In the end, his seigneur said neither.

"The Church is taking this matter seriously. Their mobilizing the Order of Kripishi in cities across Ozequn."

"Good."

"Devery asked me to send word of your arrival to the head of the Order in Arkcaster," O'Malley said. "...I haven't told them yet."

Bersk sighed and nodded. "Thank you for that. I'd rather look around the city first, before getting ordered around."

"I suspected as much, but Bersk, don't dawdle. I wouldn't be surprised if Greghan has his own channels to keep tabs on you. Lord knows the man has spite enough for you and Santa Anna."

"Greghan is the least of my worries."

"Regardless… Keep your wits about you, Bersk."

To be continued February 2023

Thank you for Reading

I hope you enjoyed reading this story as much as I enjoyed writing it.

If you did, I would massively appreciate a short review on Amazon or your favorite book website. Reviews are crucial for any author, and a starred review or even just a line or two can make a huge difference.

It's especially true for the start of a series. Thanks and I hope you enjoy the next one!

Looking for more dark fantasy stories in this universe?

The Sword of the Gray Queen is one series in a dark fantasy universe, *Eluthiya*.

Tales from Another World is an ongoing short story series containing stories about sorcerers, druids, mortals, gods, thieves, and all other manner of Terrans from all over the twin continents.

Among other stories, will be snippets of Sircius Everdeath's crusade that nearly destroyed the world! So, if you're interested, be sure to check out the ongoing series.

And if you liked the action and adventure in this story, be sure to check out the ongoing monthly serial **A Battleaxe and a Metal Arm.** It's the adventure of a lifetime… or several!

About the Sword of the Gray Queen

So, if you've read this far, you're probably curious about the origins of this story. Hopefully you read the back matter in The Sword of the Gray Queen 1.

It all came from a fan fiction idea: The Witches Kills Cereal Box Mascots.

The first installment was supposed to be Geralt going up against the Honey Smacks Dig 'Em Frog.

This installment was a hive full of Honey Nut Cheerios Bees.

See if you can guess which mascot is next!

Connect with the Author

If you want to stay up to date on the latest about Samuel's publishing news and blog, check out his website and consider signing up for his monthly newsletter.

www.SamuelFlemingBooks.com

Samuel can also be found on Reddit, Tiktok, and Facebook.

Samuel Fleming is a Science Fiction and Fantasy author.

He grew up in Maryland, spending most of his time swimming and writing. Swimming gave him a lot of time to daydream, so the two hobbies complemented each other well. Idle day dreams turned into stories, some of which stuck with him for years. These days he swims a little less and writes a lot more.

He loves a good story no matter the medium: Books, TV, video games, comics, tabletop RPG's, or podcasts—most of which he attempts to share with his wife and three kids, and occasionally on his blog.

www.ingramcontent.com/pod-product-compliance
Lightning Source LLC
Chambersburg PA
CBHW030638190726
48286CB00008B/2567